CLINT CLUSTERFUK

LUCAS PEDERSON

SEVERED PRESS
HOBART TASMANIA

CLINT CLUSTERFUK

Copyright © 2019 Lucas Pederson
Copyright © 2019 by Severed Press

WWW.SEVEREDPRESS.COM

ISBN: 978-1-922323-05-7

ONE

"Damn it, Clusterfuk," Captain Charles shouted. "Get your ass back here!"

"Sorry, Captain Constipation," I called back through the helm mic. "This birdie's gotta fly!"

I could feel the rage oozing from my helm speaker and grinned when he said, "If you don't get back in formation right now, I swear to God I'll--"

I hurtled a dead Solite. Ugly bastard. "You shouldn't swear, Captain Flaccid. Can't be good for your ticker, getting all worked up." I turned my comms off. Because, really, who wants to listen to Captain Skid Mark gibber? So rude.

Besides, I had shit to do.

Sector 13 of Dulip was a shithole. The planet itself was a shithole. The inhabitants were just as shitty. Especially the Solites. Slimy green skin. Jacked up faces no mother in their right mind would love. Mouths full of sharp teeth.

I ran directly at the horde forming in the ruins of their failed city. Hundreds of black eyes blinked in unison.

"Surprise, motherfuckers!"

I sprang from a mound of rubble, lifted my C-45 plasma rifle, and pulled the trigger. Bursts of bright blue scattered the front of the horde. Heads exploded in steaming globs of purple goo. Chests blew apart. Limbs tore from torsos.

It was fucking glorious.

By the time I landed, they were scrambling to find shelter like the bugs they were. Damn cockroaches.

"Aw," I shouted. "Y'all aren't scared of lil'ol me, are ya?" I fired the plasma rifle, turning a nearby Solite into nothing but pulverized purple pulp. "Just sayin' hi!"

I spun, crouched behind a mound of broken building. This was ridiculous. Captain Spanky back there should've charged. You can't squash bugs without actually, well, squashing the bugs. Not standing there with our thumbs up our poop chutes. Hell, I thought I could hear him bellowing from where I crouched.

He should know better, anyway.

I peeked around the mound and a series of blasts crashed into the stone inches from me. Rock shrapnel blew into my face. Thank the gods of chunky peanut butter I wore the helmet. That shit could blind a person. Saw hundreds of times with lesser soldiers. Those goobers. Of course, not everyone could be me, either. Call me gifted. In more ways than one. Wink-wink, nudge-nudge, say no more, say no more!

"Alright, cockblocks, ya asked for it," I said and rounded the mound of broken stone.

During my time behind the mound, they had massed together again.

Hehe, no one said they were smart.

I tore into them with my plasma rifle, sweeping left and right. Most were cut in half in front. I rolled behind another mound of rubble just as they opened fire. A chuckle spewed out of me. God, I love the smell of bug guts in the morning.

It wouldn't take long for them to blow the rubble apart. So…a plan. Wait, what? A plan? I shuddered. Plans sucked fuzzy donkey balls. The greatest fights were always on impulse. Plans killed you and everyone you fucking loved. Or something. Okay, probably not. But still.

The rubble quaked. Those bastards were really laying it on thick.

Fuck it.

I jumped away from my hiding spot, blasting more than a few Solites into oblivion, and sprinted to a partially intact building. They stopped shooting for a moment, giving me time to check out my surroundings a bit.

Old, blown to shit stone building. Check. A stairway leading to a nonexistent second floor. Check. A dead Solite family at my boots. Double check. Accidently stepped in Solite guts. Triple check.

The planet was in its lunar cycle. Which meant days were gloomy as all hell and nights were darker than a dead witch's cloaca.

Okay, bad analogy, but you get the idea.

It was a dark fucking planet. Miserable, really. Why the Supreme Elite hadn't blown the stupid planet into space rock was beyond my pay grade. Right then, it was around noon and dim as fuck.

Silence surrounded me.

What the shit were they doing?

I quietly moved up the stairs. Because…high ground. That, and I could look over the wall to see if the Solite bugs retreated or were trying to be tricky douchecanoes. One glance over the edge settled it.

Yup. They were being douchecanoes.

The ugly bastards were trying to surround me.

Some planet's kids…I tell ya…

I pulled an atomic grenade from my belt. The Elite's largest one. Something we weren't supposed to use unless under dire circumstances. This wasn't exactly dire, but…what the hell, right?

I yanked the pin free and let the thing tumble down the stairs. It rolled, stopping only when it struck the dead Solite family. I had ten seconds before it blew. Ten seconds before—

The stairs under me blew apart and I dropped to the floor. In a matter of seconds, before the dust settled, a Solite charged me. Too close for the rifle. I let it swing at my side and slammed an uppercut into the creature's lower jaw. I held it there and curled my right wrist. A long, serrated blade shot out of my suit's forearm and into the Solite's head. Purple and black brain matter burst from the top of the skull, including a good eight inches, hehe, of my retractable blade.

The Solite's body quivered, all six arms twitching at its side. It made a funny gurgling sound one couldn't help but laugh at. I yanked the blade out and the creature collapsed to the floor.

The atomic grenade beeped.

The five second mark.

"Ah, hell," I said and leaped out a nearby window.

I struck a pile of rubble, hated myself for not reacting sooner, and ran from the partial building.

What was the blast radius again? Twenty meters? Forty? Or—

Boom.

The blast shoved me forward. I stumbled a bit before crashing face first into gray dirt. Rocks clinked off my Elite suit. In no time, I was completely buried. Hello Darkness, my old friend…or some shit.

Times like that, you really needed to kinda stop and reevaluate your life. I mean, who in their right mind would ever want to be in the Supreme Elite? For one, they're all a bunch of macho dickwarts. For two, there was no pension. If you died, you died. Like I said…dickwarts.

I signed up to kill shit. It was just what I did. What I was good at. The *only* thing I was good at, actually. Well, besides brewing beer. I was pretty fucking fantastic at that. Still, when I joined the Supreme Elite, or, rather, SE, I thought it'd be balls to the wall fuck'em up action. Instead, I was stuck with Captain Dingleberry and all his stupid plans and protocol.

Why enlist into the most reportedly badass corps when all you did was twiddle your thumbs and shoot something every once in a while? I mean, what was the fucking point?

The SE was made to infiltrate and destroy all noncomplying entities. Both foreign and domestic. Case in point, the Solites. They weren't complying with direct orders to mine their dense listus crystals for the betterment of HOB Galaxy. Just a handful of those crystals, or so I was told, would power an entire continent for centuries. The Solites were to be paid handsomely too.

But, alas, Solites were buggy imbeciles.

I guess I couldn't blame them if they were using the crystals to better their own planet. But...they weren't. In fact, barely any crystals were ever dug up. And, if not for the Planetary Union scans, no one would have known about the rich underground fields of such a precious material and—Jesus shittin' on a cracker, why was I even thinking about all that bullshit?

I pushed out of all the dirt and rock that buried me. If not for the enhanced strength of the suit, I doubt I would've managed the task. The world was a swirl of gray when I emerged and rolled onto my back. Even with the suit, it took a lot out of me. You never knew how heavy dirt was until you found yourself buried in it. Or some shit. Whatever.

Of course, it didn't take long for Captain Syphilis and his merry band of dotards to find me. One of them helped me to my feet, which was surprising. Those meatheads (most, not all) typically cared about themselves and their bros. The other guys in the platoon, well...let's just say they were out of luck when shit hit the fan. Expendable. Y'know, just like me.

Captain Cumtowel stood in front of me, head shaking a lot, arms and hands flailing. Little did he know my helm was off. I didn't intend on turning comms back on either. Who needed the ranting and raving of a Captain who, by all accounts, should learn how to be a soldier again? Not I, said the fly.

Still...color me curious.

I turned the comms on.

"—the flying *fuck* were you thinking? You jeopardized this mission and disobeyed direct orders!" Captain Barky shook his fist at me. "You better *believe* Admiral Burlow is going to hear all about this when we return to the station." I couldn't see his face through the mirrored vision, but ten chickens to one, I bet he was all clenched teeth and popping veins. Smoke rolling out his ears like those old cartoons.

I stretched my back while he roared on and on. The suit didn't allow for much stretching so, yeah, that was pretty damn uneventful too.

"...and furthermore—"

"Right, right," I said. I clapped his shoulder on my way by. "Good talk Captain Dildo. See ya on the shuttle."

"Don't walk away when I'm talking to you, Clusterfuk!"

I made a twirling motion with my finger. "I just saved your great big crystal deal thing. Time for some shut eye. Catch ya on the flipside, dear."

"Clusterfuk! Get back here *now*! I'm not through—"

Oookay, enough of that hot shit shenanigans. I turned the comms off and moved through the platoon. To my surprise, they parted, giving me room to walk toward the shuttle. Not one of those goobers tried to stop me.

They were all still outside, doing whatever the hell Captain Buttstank barked at them, by the time I stripped out my suit and stretched out on one of the bunks.

"Yup," I said. "This is why we do it."

Seconds later, I knew nothing.

TWO

Dreams were funny things. You knew you were dreaming, and yet, also reacted to whatever world your mind catapulted your ass into for the night. Weird shit.

So, I knew I was dreaming when the creature broke through the front door of our house and tore my mom apart. I knew when its protruding maw clamped over Dad's head. I even knew when it found me hiding under my bed. All that changed, though, when I jammed the muzzle of Dad's shotgun under its lower jaw and squeezed the trigger. It changed when I was doused in the thing's greasy, red blood.

It changed when the blood soaked into my skin.

It—

Someone was kicking me. Not gently, either.

I woke to four MPs standing around my bunk.

I sat up, scratched my head, yawned. "Hey guys." I laid back down and pulled the blanket up to my chin. "Just five more minutes, k?" I closed my eyes.

"Elite Sergeant Clusterfuk," one of the MPs boomed. "You are under arrest for disobeying the direct orders of a commanding officer and putting lives in danger. On your feet, now."

I snorted. "You forgot the part where I saved the day. Nice try though, Booger Bear. Now, if you'll excuse me…" I rolled onto my side away from them.

A hand fell on my shoulder.

"Okay," I said, "look, I'm not that kind of girl. Hands off."

"Elite Sergeant Clu—"

"Get bent."

"If you do not comply, we—"

"Okay. Now you're just pissing me off."

"—will use force. You have three seconds to comply."

"And you have three seconds to suck a donkey dick. Get outta here."

They fell on me then. All groping hands and heavy mouth breathing.

"*Guh*," I said. "Rape!"

They managed to pull me out of bed. I dipped and punched the nearest douchenozzle in the face. He slammed into the wall, eyes rolling up to the whites. A trickle of blood oozed from his right nostril. He crumpled to the floor.

The other three struggled to get cuffs on me.

"Hold'im," one of the MPs said.

"Trying. He's—"

I chuckled. "I love you guys. Really."

The older of the three drew his stun gun and pointed it at me.

"But you," I told the older MP. "You're an asshole."

I swung one of the younger MPs around in front of me just as the older dude fired the stun gun. Poor kid. Foam bubbled out his mouth before he dropped like a sack of tatter tots. The older guy blinked and lowered the gun.

I kicked the other younger MP out of my way, bolted to the older one, wrenched the stun gun out of his grip and shoved him into the wall. Before he could react, I slammed the muzzle of the stun gun against his chest.

Between heavy breaths, the old guy managed, "Admiral...wants to...see you."

I lifted the stun gun away. "Well, why didn't you just say so?" I leaned against the wall beside him. "Admiral and I are tight, ya know? Good buds. How long you been doing this, old timer?"

"I-I don't follow..."

"How long you been a cop for the Elite?" I tapped the stun gun on his white helmet.

"Twenty years. About."

I nodded. "About." I smiled. "So, you're not sure?"

"Well, I...I..." He reached around his back and came out with a dagger.

In a fluid motion, I dropped the stun gun, broke his wrist, caught the dagger before it fell, and plunged it into his withered forehead. He collapsed at my feet, twitching. Damn assassins were getting sloppy these days.

"Oh my god," the remaining MP shouted. "You...you..."

"He was sent to kill me," I said and yanked the dagger from the old man's forehead. "Why are *you* here?"

He held his hands up. "J-Just to arrest you. I swear."

"Uh-huh. Who sent you?"

"No one! I just—"

A sigh blew out of me. "No one? Are you sure?"

"I swear. No one sent me here!"

I loomed over him. "Not even the Admiral?"

"Well, I...yes! He sent me. Us. He sent us! Except for that guy you killed. Never met him before today."

I slipped the tip of the dagger's blade up and down the boy's cheek. He couldn't have been older than twenty-five. "Is that right? Then why did you throw such a fit when I offed him, hmm?"

The young MP backed away, hands still raised. "I—Look, it's not like that. I thought he was who he said he was, okay? Honest!"

"That's not helpin' your case, kid," I said, pointing the dagger at him. "In fact—"

"Clusterfuk. Let him go. He's new. Started a month ago."

A woman's voice.

I grinned, gaze never straying from the young MP. "A month ago. How long has Old Man River over there been on the station?"

"A week."

"Do you ever vet these guys anymore?"

"Of course," said the woman, who sounded sexy as all hell. Sultry low tone. I fell in love instantly. "Some slip through from time to time, though. Sorry you had to deal with Ed."

I sighed and lowered the dagger. "Just make sure he's sucked out into space. Bastard doesn't deserve a funeral." I turned and gazed upon her hotness. A little meat on her bones too. I liked that. I smiled and flung the dagger over my shoulder. It clanked on the floor behind me. "Hi."

She smiled back, though not quite as enthusiastic as I was used to.

Shit. Was I losing my touch?

I *beamed* the smile directly at her, turning my charm up to eleven. "What's your name?"

And, there it was. The big smile. The giggle and slight lowering of the chin. The half-lidded eyes. The uncrossing of her arms…

"Zandra," she said, head tilting to the side a bit. "The Admiral told me about you."

I moved toward her, keeping eye contact. "Yeah? Tellin' ya all my secrets, was he?"

She shook her head. "Just that you're an arrogant asshole. But…"

"But what?" I stopped a couple feet from her. She looked up at me and bit her bottom lip. I smirked. "But what, Hotness?"

She opened her mouth then closed it again. Her smile faltered. "But, um…okay, you're messing with me now."

I snorted. "Nah. I just want to give you the full Clusterfuk." I gently stroked her cheek with the back of my hand. "I want all of you."

She sucked in a sharp breath, stepped closer, hesitated, and fell back again.

Ah, the cat and mouse game. I liked that too.

I turned to the remaining MP. "Get out."

He frowned, started forward, stopped. "I'm not supposed to—"

"Just go," Zandra spouted. "I want to talk to the Elite Sergeant alone for a second." My shriveled heart filled with even more love for the woman. "There's something going on here we need to discuss…fully." Her gaze never left mine.

The shuttle hummed around me. A sure sign we were perfectly snugged into Wilkes Station. Named after the long dead Admiral Celina Wilkes. The only Admiral who made a difference in the Milky Way Galaxy. The one who liberated so many oddball colonies. Either human, or otherwise. The very Admiral who blocked and obliterated an alien invasion that would have laid waste to at least two of the "Earth-like" planets like E-12 and especially E-23 (my home planet). There was a big, sprawling history of Admiral Wilkes and all her badass achievements, but that was for another story.

The young MP hurried out of the small bunk room, and Zandra stepped inside. The door whispered shut behind her.

"Hey, gorgeous," I said a second before she pounced on me.

We staggered a moment, her legs wrapped around me, kissing fiercely, before my thighs struck the edge of the bunk. I fell backward just as she unbuckled the belt of her black uniform. Rolling around, nibbling and kissing, we were naked in less than a handful of seconds. God, her spirit was so…vigorous.

I loved every minute of her.

All two of them.

Afterward, she kept her distance. Kind of withdrew. Her body still quivered with a residual orgasm, but she wouldn't look me in the eye anymore. Meh, happened to the best of them. Either they fell in love and got all clingy or ran away. Zandra was a runner.

We got dressed, Zandra moving much faster than I. She led the way out of the little room and to the rear hatch of the shuttle, which was wide open, giving way to the massive shuttle bay of Wilkes Station.

"Home sweet home," I said, nudging Zandra. "Hey, maybe later we can—"

"This way, Elite Sargent Clusterfuk." She started down the short platform to the bay floor.

"Well, that's just poor attitude, lady," I said, following her.

Attendants, rotating flight crews, fighting platoons, and god knew who else bustled every which way like scurrying ants. It was fucking maddening if you sat and watched for too long. That's why I kept my attention on Zandra. Which also surprised me. I hated relationships, and yet, there I was, practically trying to hump her leg like a sexually frustrated dog.

We made a b-line for a set of guarded double doors. Big, thick metal. Sealed. Where the "important" people hung out, in other words.

I skipped a bit beside Zandra. "We're off to see the Admiral. The wonderful Admiral of Wilkes!"

She shot a glare at me. "Are you always an idiot?"

I skidded to a stop, slapped a hand over my heart. "Gasp! The Winter Witch speaks!"

She walked faster.

"Hey! Wait up, sweet'n'sexy sauce!"

She stopped and spun on me. "Do you ever shut up?"

"Well, there was that one time with the ballgag." I shook my head. "But that's a whole other can of worms we probably shouldn't get into surrounded by strangers." I nodded. "Hey Phil."

A lanky, bald man walking by rolled his eyes and continued on. Well, fuck you too, Phil.

"You're being obnoxious," Zandra whisper-growled at me. "Just because we…whatever. Doesn't mean I want to be with you again."

I smirked. "You're kinda sexy when you get all pissy. How 'bout we go back to the shuttle and—"

"You're a sick pig," she said, turned and stormed toward the tall double doors.

I blinked. "Is that a suckling pig, or just your average ham?"

She didn't respond and was already talking with the guards when I caught up to her.

"Guys, I need advice here," I said. "If, say, you bang a hot girl like this and she treats you like dog shit on the bottom of your boot, what would you do?"

"Ignore him," Zandra told the guards. "He's heading for a court martial."

"Whoa, whoa, WHOA! Stop. Pause." I stepped between the guards and Zandra and faced her. "What the shit are you talkin' about?"

She cocked a dark eyebrow. "Really? Why else would MPs be waking you up?"

"Okay, for one, they weren't all MPs. For two, what the *shit*?"

"Permission granted, Lieutenant Rowe," one of the guards spoke behind me. "You may proceed with the prisoner."

"Prisoner—what the ever-loving *shitnuggets*?" I glanced from Zandra to the guard and back again. "You got the wrong guy. I was framed!"

Zandra sighed. "Let's go." She rushed forward once the doors hissed open.

I turned and glanced at the guards. "Never bang the fiery ones, my dudes. They're nothin' but trouble after—"

"Clusterfuk," Zandra shouted. "Move your feet!"

I snorted. "See what I mean?" I quickly caught up to her. "Why am I being court martialed, by the way? It's my face, isn't it? Too perfect the big guys can't handle the handsome? Amiright?"

She shook her head. "You don't remember killing six of your platoon during your little atomic grenade spectacle?"

I stopped walking. My heart thudded. "What?"

Still walking, she said, "You disobeyed direct orders, and, because of that, six of our men were killed." She didn't turn around. "Your reckless behavior has been unchecked for far too long. Up until now, none of our own died because of your stupidity. Time to face the consequences."

I frowned, once more catching up to her. We walked down a long, white corridor. "So, if you knew all that, why'd we do it?"

She chuckled. "That's none of your business."

"None of my—look, lady, you came onto me first."

Zandra didn't respond. She didn't pause her stride. What she did was forge ahead until we came to another set of big double doors. Zandra was much stronger than some women I encountered. Maybe that's why I wanted to hump her leg? Heh…no (yes). *Anyway,* she placed a thumb on a pad near the double doors. They whispered open so much more smoothly than the first set. Guess it paid to be powerful. Outside was minor securities for the soldiers and crew. Inside, however…

I fell quiet and followed Zandra around. I'd never been in that part of Wilkes so I took it all in. The polished steel walls. The fake marble floors were waxed shiny. At least I assumed they were fake. The cold, bright inlaid lights dotting the ceilings. All of it made me cringe. Like walking around in a high-end hospital. Sterile and inhuman. Simply a place, nothing more.

God…I needed out of there.

I brushed by Zandra.

"Hey," she said.

"Let's get this over with, eh? Where are all the doors, anyway?"

"This is the scanning hall, jackass."

I chuckled. "So…we're being watched right now?"

"Bodies are being scanned for anything alien, weapons, and whatever the MSTs find."

"Oh, well in that case…" I flipped off the walls, ceiling and floor.

MST meant Military Scanning Team. A group of assholes being assholes, who paraded around thinking they're more important than every guy out there risking their lives for whatever stupid cause the Governs deemed critical. If they didn't like you, they could set an alarm, plant something on you and get you tossed into The Pit. The most infamous prison planet floating around the Milky Way.

With me, however…heh, let 'em try.

"If you don't fall back, I'll be forced to stun you," Zandra said.

"Kinky."

"I'm serious, Clusterfuk."

"Oh, stop. Not like I'm going anywhere. Ya got the MST cockblocks and I have no fucking clue where we are right now."

"There will be doors up ahead. The MSTs will let us through."

I grunted. "Yeah? Well…" I spun in a circle. "They're all a bunch of douchenozzles and couldn't fight their way through a wall of tissue paper!"

"Clint," Zandra said. "That's enough. They—"

I continued walking, arms spread out on either side. "Here douchey, douchey, douchey."

A loud bray blared through the hall.

"Goddamn it, Clusterfuk," Zandra said, voice nearly a growl.

"Remain where you are," a deep voice commanded. "Hands on top of your head. Prepare for inspection."

"Oh, no," I spouted. "Not the MSTs! Whatever shall I do?"

Sometimes I had a method to my madness.

But not that day.

I was just bored.

And I didn't stop walking. Nor did I place my hands on my head. I mean, really? They thought that tactic worked for alien smugglers, or whatever? Dumbasses.

The doors Zandra was talking about were no more than thirty feet in front of me.

"Clint," Zandra shouted. "Stop and comply! They shoot to kill if you don't comply."

"Yeah, well," I said, "They gotta shoot me first."

"Oh my god," Zandra said. "It's all true. You *are* crazy."

I stopped, spun around, and pressed a finger to my pursed lips. "Shh. Don't let the cat outta the bag, darlin'."

When I turned toward the doors, I was greeted with six MTS's. All heavily geared up and armed. Helmets and everything.

I smiled. "Now, *there* are some guys who take their job just a tad too seriously." I rushed toward them. "Hi fellas!"

They opened fire.

I caught one in the gut but managed to sidestep and avoid the rest. Nuke-frags. Of *course* it was Nuke-frags. Burned like hell just took a massive dump all over my stomach. Fire and brimstone, yadda-yadda.

I sprinted full speed at them and laughed when they tried backing through the doorway all at once.

"Aw," I shouted. "Don't go! It's playtime!"

They managed to squeeze through the doorway.

I reached out, grabbed one of the bastards' arms, and yanked him forward just as the doors closed. Blood spurted then splashed the doors, floor, and spattered my chest. I stumbled backward, the dude's arm in my hand. I turned it right side up and waved it at a small, black lens in the wall to my left.

"Oh my god," Zandra said behind me. She sounded out of breath. "You're sick."

"What's sick is this dude's fingernails." I whirled and flapped the hand at her. "Just look at all the dirt under'em."

She frowned, shook her head. "You need help. I thought, at first, it was just an act. But…this…"

I tossed the arm aside and winked. "Rough childhood. Daddy was a meth-head and Mommy was a whore." A lie, but, oh well. Sometimes my mouth worked faster than my brain. Happened a lot.

Zandra's frown deepened. "How did you ever get into the Elite Supreme?"

I favored her with a shrug. "I just kinda happen to be good at killing things."

"Oh."

I winked. "It's a gift."

Zandra rolled her eyes and stepped toward the doors. "This is Lieutenant Rowe requesting entry. Elite Sargent Clusterfuk is my prisoner. We have orders to meet with the Admiral and his council."

A long pause followed. So long, I almost said fuck it and beat down the doors. I only had so much patience. The older I got, the less that sloshed in the reservoir of patience. That motherfucker was damn near dry, too.

The doors opened and we walked through. In their glassed-in room stood the MST cowards. A couple were trying to tie a tourniquet on the guy who lost an arm. Blood slathered the floor Zandra and I walked through.

"Better make it good'n'tight," I told them while we passed. "He lost a lot of blood already. Another five minutes and he could be dead."

"Fuck you," one of the MSTs bellowed.

"I'm kinda busy right now," I said. "But maybe later, honeybun!"

Zandra grabbed my arm and pulled me onward. The MST flipped me off. Bastard. I stuck my tongue out, started back to beat his ass, but Zandra yanked me around. Before long we came to another goddamn set of big goddamn doors. Because, of course we did. That's all the place seemed to be. Halls and big doors. It was getting pretty fucking boring. Guess I shouldn't have expected more from a bunch of loose skin bags, but, ya know…one held out hope.

Hope, though, never got anything done. Just a crutch people leaned on. Good or bad, it was bullshit.

The new set of big doors whispered open, giving way, to my surprise, a very large room lined with wooden benches and dozens of men and women sitting in them. Kinda cute how proper they all appeared. Bet more than one of them helped authorize the murder of millions.

Zandra stopped and turned to me. "If you don't screw it up, they might be lenient. You've done more good than bad according to the records. Just walk up to the bench and stand still. Let them say their piece and accept their offer."

A snort flew out of me. "I think we passed a bathroom back there. Wanna have one last romp before I—"

The slap came so fast even I didn't have time to react. Which was something I wasn't used to. Usually, I saw those things coming, heh. Zandra was a force I hadn't encountered before. And I kinda liked it.

"If you don't want them to kill you," she said, "shut up and accept their punishment. Just…don't say anything at all."

I smiled. "Aw, you *do* love me!"

She blinked, shook her head. "My god, you really are an idiot."

"Love you too, darlin'."

I patted her shoulder and entered the chamber of, "We seal your fate", Martial Court. So much for speaking with the Admiral beforehand. Ah, well…

I walked down a long, crimson carpet all the way to the looming Head of Court. A massive wooden structure too close to a pulpit for my liking. Glowering down at me were three old men and three old women. In the middle, in his black uniform decked out with shiny medals, gray hair flat on his head, sat the Admiral. I didn't even know his name. Hell, I didn't think anyone did until…

"Elite Sargent Clusterfuk. I am Admiral Burlow." He leaned forward a bit. "And, let me tell you, I wish we were meeting under other circumstances."

I opened my mouth and caught myself. There it went again. Flapping before my brain engaged. Sigh. I snapped my mouth shut. Nodded.

Well, at least I knew the dude's name. Right?

"As I am sure you're aware," Admiral Burlow continued, "You are here for charges on abandoning your platoon, defying a superior officer's direct orders, and endangering the lives of not just your platoon, but the humans who live on Dulip. As I am sure you are also aware, Dulip, especially Sector 13 and the Solite society, are major trades of ours. They have many resources to better our survival on Earth and Earth Two."

I was kinda aware of all that, but really didn't care. Earth was turning into a cesspool— much like Dulip—quicker than anyone wanted to admit. And Earth Two, although much larger than Earth, was a pain in the ass to settle on due to shifting magnetic plates under the crust. Or something like that. Science wasn't my thing.

"The charges," Admiral Burlow said, "are rather alarming, Clusterfuk. For all your great accomplishments with the Supreme Elite, you have dashed it all to ashes with your behavior in Sector 13. And, quite frankly, I am severely saddened and disappointed in you."

"Thanks, Dad," I spouted and slapped myself. Literally. "Sorry, Admiral."

He didn't flinch. "Your mouth has gotten you in trouble before. I read hundreds of reports over the couple of years you joined the team and the reports of your last team, Skull Daggers. I knew you had a smartass mouth on you but accepted your application. Why? Because, up until Sector 13, you at least worked with your team. You didn't go rogue for long and followed orders...for the most part."

Jumpin' Jesus on a lily pad. How watered down were those reports from Skull Daggers? I remembered going off on my own because of incompetent leaderships dozens of times. Like Captain Shit-Splatter on Sector 13. When the bastards aren't gonna back down and won't be peaceful...fuck'em. Either scare them enough to send them running, or kill'em all.

Admiral Burlow straightened. "Elite Sargent Clusterfuk, I hereby strip you of your stripes and relocate you to Earth."

"What the *fuck*? Listen, cockknock—"

"I am not finished," the Admiral boomed. He sighed. "However, you have been an important asset to every team and platoon you were a part of. It does my heart good to know that you are a shining star among the Intergalactic Military. For this, you will also be sent to do good on Earth."

I blinked. "What are you talking about?"

He slammed his gavel. "From this moment forward, you are no longer Elite Sargent Clusterfuk. This discharge is not an honorable one and I wish you luck in your appointed profession on Earth." His heavily lined face softened a bit. "For what it's worth, thank you for your service."

He slammed the gavel again and a shock of…something…blasted through me.

Darkness clouded in.

THREE

Thud.

The darkness didn't recede all at once, rather, it lingered a bit along the fringes of reality. I was aware of two things, though.

I laid on my right side, the sun which spilled over my fingers the color of whiskey.

And, my head hurt like hell. Like a dozen rubber mallets just pounding away at my stupid skull.

"He's awake, mate."

I tried to roll onto my back but couldn't move. Paralyzed? Was that my punishment? Did those motherfuckers really—

"About time. The dickhead's been asleep for three days."

Three days? What the *shit*? And what were those accents? Sounded oddly familiar…

"They said he'd be out for a couple days, mate. Won't be able to move hours after."

"Christ, he's looking at me!"

Was I? Shit, all I could see was the whiskey color of the sun on my fingers. Weird.

"Shut up, cunt. He's got the wandering eye. They told us that, remember? Just leave'im be till the shock wears off."

A long pause followed, then, "You think he can hear us?"

"Fuck knows. Leave'im be. We'll sort it out later."

My eyelids dipped shut and darkness crowded in once more.

Don't do drugs, kids…

***

When I woke up the second time, I managed to roll onto my back and stared at a high, vaulted ceiling. I was in a bed, a light blanket shrouding me. The day was well past the deep whiskey color warming my fingers from before.

It was as bright as a goddamn nuclear bomb. Probably just as hot too.

I wiped sweat from my forehead and tried to sit up. The first couple attempts resulted in otherwise comical crappie flops. Never in my life had I felt so physically useless. Not happening again. That shit sucked slimy salamander nuts. If ever I got stood in front of old people to discuss my fate, I'd just kill'em. At least I wouldn't have to suffer the indignity of being man-mush and flopping around like a dying fish.

Finally, I managed to sit, every breath I took burned. Now, what the fuck was *that* about? Gods of steaming shit, what did they do to me? My mouth felt like I just got off a three-day bender. Old, dry carpet, with a puke stain or four. I needed water, or beer. Or both? Both.

My legs were proverbial rotten logs. Couldn't move the bastards no matter how much I tried. I felt them, just…nothing worked. So weird.

I was just getting my idiot legs kind of working when a lanky, tall man with deeply tanned, leathery skin sauntered into the room. He held a large glass of water with ice cubes floating near the top and a straw in the other hand. My gaze narrowed on the beads of condensation slipping down the glass. If it was closer, I probably would've licked the damn glass like a thirsty dog.

"You're awake," the man said, not smiling. "Thought you were gonna be cactus for a few days, there." He walked to the side of the bed and plunked the straw into the water. "They said you'd be a thirsty bloke when you woke up." He held the glass out toward me.

I leaned, sucked a trickle of water down. I was too dry. Couldn't seal my lips fully around the straw. But, after a couple more attempts, I managed to suck down some good gulps. By the fifth gulp, I swished my barren mouth with water and swallowed. I did that a few more times before finally backing away from the straw. I knew I couldn't get too crazy. If I drank too much after being dehydrated it could really fuck me up.

So, I leaned back, letting the water settle a bit. "Ca—" It came out more like a squeak. I shook my head and cleared my throat. Tried again. "Cactus?"

The man grunted. A thin smile spread on his weathered face. "An American, ay?"

"Uh, kinda. Why'd you call me a cactus? I don't have any needles, jackass."

He rolled his eyes. "I have to give ya lessons on bein' an Aussie now? Cactus. Like dead or in a bad way, ya cunt."

I snorted. "They sent me to Australia? And don't call me cunt, cunt."

"Hold this." The man pointed at the glass of water. "I got shit to do."

"Well…excuse me, cockbiter." I grabbed the glass of water from him, sloshing a bit on the bed. I waved a hand at him. "Take a hike, Crocodile Dundee."

He spat at me, missing, thankfully, and stormed out.

I sat back in bed and drank my water, wondering what kind of fuckery Admiral Burlow and his elderly council of hemorrhoids put me in.

Once the water was finished, I placed the glass on a bedside table and attempted to get out of bed. My legs seemed to be working okay. The floor, cool on my bare feet, I tried standing. And I did, for a second or two, then fell back onto the bed.

"Goddamn it," I said.

"Paul said you were awake," a smooth, yet still very Australian voice spoke to my left.

I turned enough to watch a shorter, slightly older man walk toward me. He had a red, bulbous nose and bright blue eyes. His hair was covered by a tan cattleman hat. His smile was big, genuine, almost grandfatherly. He might've been in his early sixties, by the look.

"G'day."

"Yeah," I said. "Paul is an asshole."

The older man chuckled. "Fuckin' prick, ain't he?" He held out a hand. "Rick."

I blew out a breath and turned my head away. "Christ, man. You smell like a catfish bathing in the sun. And not in a sexy way."

Rick chuckled some more. "Don't get many showers out here in the bush."

"Are you like…my parole officer or something?"

The older man's smile faded. "Nah. You been sent to help us out. Can come and go as you please. We're just hired to take care of you and offer you a job."

I frowned. "A job? What kinda job?"

With a pat on my shoulder, Rick snorted and said, "Once you're back on your pins, we'll talk about it."

"Eh, no. Let's talk about it now. I hate surprises, jackass."

He shrugged, shook his head and sat down beside me. "Well, we hunt roos."

I blinked. "Roos?"

"That's right, you're a Yank. I forgot you're not up to speed with our lingo." He took off his hat and tossed it on the bed. "Short for kangaroos." A smile stretched his mouth wide. "Except these things are bloody rabid."

"Rabid—okay, what kinda fuckery *is* this?"

"Like the rest of Earth," Rick said, "Australia has been turned upside down. A new strain of rabies has spread through the continent, ya know? A few of us were hired to weed out the disease and burn it until the rabies is gone. Unfortunately, what you might know is kangaroos, have been the main carriers."

"Sounds like loads of fun. How long you been doing this?"

Rick shrugged. "Almost fifteen years now."

I whistled. "Holy shit. Really? And the rabies shit isn't gone? The hell you all doin'? Yanking each other's bomb-pops instead of hunting?"

Rick's eyes narrowed. "How'd you know, mate?" He grinned. "Truth is, the disease ain't like anything anyone has ever seen. Before this, rabies never existed here. Then the world changed. It's rabies, but it's mutated, according to scientists. It's highly aggressive. The animals aren't all rage. They're smart. Harder to hunt 'cause they really *think*."

"Ever try napalm?" I tried standing again and failed. I slumped on the bed. "Might be a better way of killin' the fuckers off." I shook my head. "Wait, doesn't rabies practically melt the brain? Thought I read that somewhere. Heard it? Shit, maybe my dog from childhood had rabies. Ya can't have super smart and fast and rabies together. Just doesn't work, old fella."

"I'm fifty-four," Rick said. "Old to you, I suppose." He squinted at me. "You learned how to shave yet?" That mischievous twinkle returned to his eyes. "Anyway, how long you been away from Earth, mate?"

It took me a moment. "Um, about twenty years. I somehow got sent to the Venera Station. Ya know, the first real space station before Earth finally went to shit. I was sixteen when they found Earth Two."

Rick nodded. "Well, then." He brought a flask, unscrewed the cap and sucked down whatever was inside. When he stopped, I caught a whiff and grinned.

Whiskey.

My new friend, it appeared, liked a good snort here and there. Shit…me too.

I grabbed the flask from him and sucked down a swig. It burned a bit. Been awhile since I had real Earth whiskey. The heat trickled down my throat and settled in my stomach, blossoming into my bloodstream. I almost forgot how absolutely fucking wonderful that felt. No booze in all the galaxies really compared to Earth's booze.

Another swig, and I handed the flask back to Rick.

He capped and pocketed it. "I guess they're not exactly smarter, though extremely aggressive. So much…they *appear* smarter, if that makes sense?"

I thought about it. "Uh, no. Doesn't make sense at all, dude."

Rick sighed. "That's right, I forgot you only climbed out of nappies last year." He clapped his hands down on his bony knees and stood. "Only way for you to bloody know is for you to see it yourself, mate."

I held up a hand. "Hey now, let's not get too crazy. I just woke up."

The older man laughed, which would mark exactly six people who laughed at something I said. Not including my own mother. And grandmother. And aunt. Shut up.

I shook it off and tried to stand again. I wobbled like a whore with a peg leg, though finally got it done. See kids? Never give up. Or some shit.

I shambled toward the door on legs like pillars of gelatin. I leaned on the doorjamb a bit and shot a glance over my shoulder. "I'm kinda hungry."

Rick bounced off the bed and blew by me. "Right, right. This way."

I tottered at his passing, nearly biffed it, caught myself. Once I was steady, I glared in Rick's general direction. "Hey, thanks for the help Crocodile Dun-ASS!" I didn't know if he heard me or not and didn't care.

All my focus returned to walking. Something as easy as breathing, and yet...

I stumbled over the threshold. "Fucker." My left foot dragged a bit sending me into a wall. "Bastard." I staggered away from the wall, arms pinwheeling some, like a drunk and crashed into a small table. Both I and the table collapsed to the floor. I rolled onto my back, puffing out my cheeks. "Well, shit."

"Ah, hell," Rick said and knelt beside. "I could've brought the tucker to you, mate."

"Well," I said, staring at a water stained ceiling. "That would've been fuckin' good to know, Rick."

"Here," Rick said, "Let's get you back to bed."

I waved him away. "Back off wrinkly balls." I struggled to sit up, though made it. "I've been in bed long enough."

"Right, then." Rick stood. "I'll get your bum-nuts and murphy's ready." He hurried off.

I frowned. "Bum-nuts and what the *shit*?"

Eventually, I gained my feet and sort of ping-ponged my ass down the short hall to an open kitchen where I was smacked in the face with the familiar aromas of fried eggs and hash-browns. My stomach groaned. I couldn't even remember the last time I ate real eggs and hash-browns. But...what the hell were bum-nuts and murphy's anyway? I better get eggs and fucking hash-browns, damn it. I swear, if they murdered a bum just to feed me his nuts…

Rick swooped around the kitchen humming a weird tune under his breath. He flipped hash-browns in one skillet, then flipped eggs in another. The stove itself appeared as old as dirt. Black, wood burning, and made the kitchen ten times hotter than it had any right to be. None of that seemed to bother Ol' Rick, however. Older, he might have been, but damn, the guy could move with the grace of a twenty-five-year old dancer. Not that I ever knew any twenty-five-year old dancers, but still…

At the table, another older man sat with a cup of coffee near to his liver spotted hand. Older. Yes. Like seven times older than Rick. And the old dude stared at me with his steely gray eyes.

I staggered to the table and sat down across from him.

He hooked the handle of his coffee cup and took a long swig before placing it gently on the table. His gray eyes never strayed from me.

Yup. I knew an asshole when I saw one. And that old bastard was a true and through asshole.

Still, I tried being nice. It felt weird, though. Like a bowl of chocolate pudding running down my navel weird.

"Hey," I told the old timer. "How's it goin'?"

One of his bushy white eyebrows rose. "The fuck are you?"

I raised my own eyebrow in return. "The fuck are you, *sir*?" Because, elder and all.

He leaned back, side-eyeing me. "American bloke? Haven't seen one in twenty years."

"Yeah, well, you know us American blokes. We just drop outta the sky when you least expect it and lay waste to everything you ever loved." I snapped my fingers. "If ya think about it, we're kinda like dragons!"

To my surprise, the old man grunted. "Got a name?"

I sighed. "I dunno. Maybe? Mom kept calling me something over and over, but I just can't—It's Clint Clusterfuk."

The old man drank his coffee, placed the cup down. "Clusterfuk, huh?"

I shrugged. "It's Norwegian."

He squinted at me. "You tellin' me your last name is truly Clusterfuk, mate?"

"Uh…not Cluster*fuck*, as you're pronouncing it. Here, lemme help ya out. It's Clooster—fook."

The old timer shook his head. "That's not how you said it."

I leaned back in my chair. "Do you want me to smash that coffee cup over your bald head? Because that's how you get a coffee cup smashed over your head."

He shifted in his chair, pointed a crooked finger at me—

"Now then," Rick said and slid a plate of over-easy eggs and crispy hash-browns (though thicker than any hash-brown I was used to) in front of me and the old man. "You both need ya strength. So, eat up."

I pointed at the old man. "*He* needs to be put back in his crypt."

The old man chuckled, dragging the plate closer to him. "I like this one."

"Me too," I said. "I'm pretty sure I'm awesome." I scooped a forkful of eggs and hash-brown into my mouth, taste buds igniting in a frenzy of marvel. Of remembrance. Too many years had passed for me to enjoy a simple plate of eggs and hash-browns. "So," I said after swallowing. "What the shit are bum-nuts and murphy's, by the way?"

Rick and the old man exchanged a glance and barked laughter.

I chuckled along, humorlessly, until they quieted down.

"No. Seriously…the hell are those?"

Rick pointed at my plate. "You're eating it, mate."

I paused, another forkful an inch from my mouth. "Asshole says what?"

"What?" Rick said. He tapped the edge of the plate with a less than manicured finger. "It might be the arvo, but we make bum-nuts and murphy's every meal."

"Arvo?" I lowered the fork and frowned at Rick. "Look, if ya don't start speaking English, I'm gonna kick ya in *your* bum-nuts."

The old man chuckled, shook his head and ate his food. Rick, on the other hand, appeared a little hurt. His wrinkly face drooped. Eyes got all sad.

"Arvo means," Rick said, turned toward the stove, "afternoon. Bum-nuts are what we call eggs. Murphy's are potatoes." He dropped one of the skillets into the sink and walked out.

I leaned back in my chair and whistled. "Got a temper on'im, doesn't he?"

The old man leveled his pale, blue eyes on me. "Rick's a good bloke. I should know. He's my son."

I sighed. "Sorry." I meant it, god help me. And I needed things not to get crazy. I had no quarrel with these folks. And Rick actually treated me great until I pushed too far.

Like I said, sometimes my mouth flapped before my brain caught up. Most of the time, I didn't care. Then, however…with Rick…

I shook the weird feelings off.

The old man snorted. "Nah. Gave me a bit of a snicker. Rick has always been a bloody softy. Cares too much. In the bush, soft blokes are cactus. But Rick…" He waved one of his liver spotted hands. "He has some switch. Lovely one second, a fuckin' hungry croc the next."

I stared at him for a long time. Finally, I blinked. "I have no idea what you just said, but coolbeans!" I shot him a thumbs up.

He rolled his eyes. "Fuckin' Yanks…"

We ate our bum-nuts and murphy's until our plates were clean. I gulped down a glass of water Rick must've placed nearby without me noticing. Sneaky bloke. Wait? Gah! I was already talking in my noggin like an Aussie. Mental slap.

"What's your name, old timer?"

He finished off his coffee and slammed the cup onto the table. "Roland. They call me Ro out there." He cocked a bent thumb over his narrow shoulder.

"Ro," I said, letting the name filter into my mental files.

"Yup." He stood, stretched. His back made a long series of crackles. He slumped a bit, sighed and gestured for me to follow him. "Time to get to work, cunt."

"Hey now, Ro…I thought we were friends." I stepped beside him. Legs still feeling messed up. "What's with all the cunt business? And I don't mean prostitution."

"You have a lot to learn 'bout Aussies, Clusterfuk. Just gotta shut that yapper long enough to listen."

We stepped out of the kitchen and into a large foyer-like area. "You Aussies are so weird."

Ro chuckled. "You have no idea, mate."

Folded neatly on one of the benches were a set of clothes. Military grade cargo pants, plain black t-shirt, plain black long-sleeved shirt, socks, black boots.

"Yeah," Ro said. "Those are yours."

I got dressed without a word. Everything fit. How the shit did they know my sizes? I blamed that old asshole in the sky, Admiral Burlow. Just thinking about his name triggered rage.

Somehow…someway, I was going to punch a hole in his decrepit chest.

"Vest over there," Ro said, nodding to a coatrack near the door. "Guns are outside."

I slipped the cargo vest on and grinned. "Guns. Now we're talkin'."

We ventured outside and I about burst into flames like a fucking vampire. The sun slashed into my eyes. A burning blade. The heat sunk its fiery claws into my skin. I staggered a bit.

"Bloody hot t'day," Ro mused. He gave me a strong pat on the back. "It'll cool off t'night. This way."

Little did the old bastard know, I was struggling to simply breathe. I needed a goddamn mech suit here. Something. Anything. The heat was ridiculous. I almost went back inside to cook some more bum-nuts.

Curiosity got the best of me, though. I straightened, opened my eyes to slits and shuffled forward. My legs were waking up, finally. Working, not quite at full strength, but enough to carry me along.

My eyes soon adjusted to the scalding bright hell of the sun and before I knew it, I stood with Ro in front of two black Land Cruisers.

Rick hurried out of a shed to my right while Paul burst through the door of another shed to my left. I tensed a bit. I'd been double-crossed before and—

"We're meeting up with Scuz," Paul announced, shooting me a glare. "This fucker ready to go?"

Rick nodded. "Yeah." He didn't give me the hateful glare Paul did but, rather, something sad. "Should be fully functional now."

"Okay," I spouted. "First off, I have a name. Second off, I'm not a fuckin' robot. So, you can stick that functional shit right up both your asses."

Ro fetched a heavy sigh. Rick lowered his head.

Paul, however, stormed toward me. "The fuck is your problem, ya little prick?"

I straightened. "My problem?" I stepped to meet him head on. We stood no closer than four inches from each other. "My *problem* is you look like a burlap sack fucked a Koala and had a baby."

Paul yanked his Bowie knife out and shot it between us. He turned it back and forth, so the steel glinted in the sun. "I could gut you right here and now, boy. And no one would ever know."

I smiled. "Well, aren't you just adorable."

His lined, deeply tanned face sneered. "Don't believe me?"

"Oh," I said, "I believe you. Those fucknuts up there really don't care. But—"

I grabbed his wrist, fingertips digging into a pressure point. His hand fell limp and with my other hand I snatched the knife. I swung him around, snugging the sharp edge of the blade against his throat. The knife was probably ridiculously sharp, knowing them, so I didn't press very hard. Even so, he fell limp in my arms and quickly drew the knife blade away. Killing him might have been better, but...ya know....

He dropped from my arms and collapsed into the reddish dirt, whimpering.

I gave Ro and Rick a glance. "What? I used to be an Elite Sargent for the Supreme Elite. I know things…"

Rick, from out of nowhere, smiled. "I think you should be up the front."

I nodded. "Good decision." I dropped the knife and it plopped in the dirt by Paul's shuddery body. "Let's do this. Whatever *this* is."

Rick smiled the tiniest bit. "We're hunting roos, like I said."

"Oh," I said. "Right. The fucked up rabid ones. Gotcha." I helped Paul to his feet and patted his shoulder. "You're okay."

He swayed, nodded, and stumbled to the Land Cruiser on the right. He shot me a glance before finally climbing into the vehicle.

Before I went to get into the vehicle on the left, Rick stopped me.

His grip firm around my forearm. "Careful with Paul. That lovely cunt has been known to kill a man."

I grunted. "Yeah, well…I'm not that easy to kill either." I pulled out of his grip and got in the four-wheel drive opposite Paul.

FOUR

"Guns are in the back," Ro said while the elderly Land Cruiser jostled and creaked over the rocky, uneven terrain. "We only use two types. The big one and the small one."

"The big one…and the small—what the hell you yammering on about now, Ro?"

Ro let go a long, gravelly sigh. His hands gripped the steering wheel, knuckles white.

I slapped myself. "Bad Clusterfuk. *Bad*!" I turned fully in my seat to the old man. "My mouth gets ahead of me. What kinda guns? I doubt they're plasma."

His hands eased on the wheel a bit. He took a few slow breaths. Finally, he said, "Don't know what plasma is. Got an elephant rifle and a thirty-oh six."

It took me a second to flip through my mental catalogue of guns. I snapped my fingers when I envisioned the guns. But…

"Wait, you need an elephant gun for kangaroos?"

"Yeah," Ro said. "Big roos out here."

"As big as an elephant?"

"Nah." He shot me a glance. "Been doin' this since I was a lad. We got a way we do it. You'll see."

I nodded, returning my attention to the tan, rocky Australian outback. At least I thought it was the outback. Bush? Well…there were a couple trees here and there, but…

The day died, leaking into dusk and, eventually, night. Darkness shrouded us. A darkness so thick, the Land Cruiser's headlights barely penetrated it. So, this would be my new life, eh? Hunting down rabid kangaroos and living out in the bush with three touchy dudes. Well, except for Ro. Ro was cool shit.

Eventually, the near barren land filled in a bit (just a bit) with some trees. In the headlights' glare, the tan ground turned green.

"Let Paul be," Ro said out of nowhere.

"Huh?"

"He's my youngest son and has the worst temper. But, he's our hunter. That prick can find the roos like no one. We, even I, follow his lead. So should you."

"I lead myself, thanks. Paul doesn't scare me."

"He should. He killed more than a couple men who got on his bad side."

I grinned, still facing the windshield. "All I'm sayin', is…he better not get on *my* bad side." I looked at the old man. "I don't take orders well, unless I respect the one giving the orders. So far, I don't respect that goober."

Ro chuckled. "You will after tonight."

I rolled my eyes. "Yeah. Sure, old timer."

Over the radio fixed just under the rearview mirror, Paul said, "Bastards gotta be less than a click to the west. They're migrating in their usual patterns."

I cocked an eyebrow. "Well, he sounds smarter than he looks."

Ro opened his mouth to say something when Paul said, "Follow me, Pop. We'll need to park up and go on foot this time."

Ro sighed. He tapped the receiver button twice. Clearly their own way of communication. Two for yes. One for no. Or some shit.

"We go walkabout through the bush," Ro said, "it gets very dangerous. There are more things out there than rabid roos this time'o'night."

"More things?" I asked.

"The fuckin' Nuclear War found its way to us," Ro said, turning the wheel to follow Paul's four-wheel-drive. "Radiation. Chemicals. Fallout. Diseases. It all found a jet stream and got us. Probably why we have rabies when we never did before. I don't know. All that shit, it coated everything. The next generation of koala became aggressive bastards. We used to take the piss out of tourists by telling them about drop bears. Turns out it's not a joke anymore. Those koalas are mad cunts that killed hundreds of people before we drove them back into the bush and set up walls around the cities." He shook his head. "Reports said they killed each other off, but we found an entire family unit out here. They hunt you. Follow you around. One could be a foot away and you'd never know. But they're rare now. Gotta be on lookout for the Bunyip."

I shook my head. "Wait. What's Bunyip?"

"S'posed to be mythical. But after the War…they came out of the rivers and ate whatever was near. We shot one. Last year. Big bastard. Big as a fuckin' elephant, you might say."

I laughed. Couldn't help myself. "Big as an elephant, huh? Why did it take nuclear fallout and climate changes, and whatever the hell else turned Earth into a piss stain, before these things were seen? I mean…if there's a creature as big as an elephant hiding in the rivers, wouldn't there be evidence before shit hit the fan?"

Ro shrugged. "Plenty of evidence with our Aboriginal friends. Stories, but I never knew an Abo to lie."

"Uh-huh," I said. "So, you shot one and none of you took a picture or had it stuffed or anything?" I sighed. "I dunno, Ro, sounding a little fishy to me."

He actually chuckled at that. "We get back and I'll give you a look."

Paul rolled to a stop behind a thicket and Ro pulled up next to him, cutting the engine.

The old man gave my arm a pat. "Let's go huntin', mate."

Getting out of the Land Cruiser, I said, "Better get to kill a Bunyip, or I'm leaving."

***

I knew Australia was hot. Okay, no I didn't. I *heard* Australia was hot. But, Christ sloggin' through a pool of tepid shit, it really was hot. Even at night. The air still held the sun's scorch.

Either that or I was just a wuss.

Probably a wuss.

But, shit, it was fucking hot.

"Careful the browns out here, ya cunts," Paul said as we trudged through thigh-high grasses.

I snapped a look at Ro. We each wore headlamps and I got him good with my glare. He waved me away and I looked down.

"What's he talking about?" I asked.

"Ya aren't very smart, are ya?" Paul muttered.

"Eat donkey cock," I spouted.

"You first, mate."

I rushed toward him, but Rick and Ro stopped me. Barely. I could've tossed them both aside like ragdolls but decided last minute against it. Paul would get his someday, though. The bastard.

Paul chuckled and continued walking.

"Browns are snakes," Rick said, letting me go. "Bloody venomous snakes that will kill you within minutes."

"Oh," I said, straightening. "Well, someone could've fuckin' said so. Why are you all so goddamn cryptic?"

Rick and Ro exchanged a glance, laughed a bit and followed Paul. They left me there glowering at their backs.

I sighed, looked around, skin crawling. Snakes. I forgot Australia was the place that constantly wanted to kill you. Australia and Africa. The twins of continental death. True story. But snakes…I fucking hated snakes. Toss me in a pool of crocodiles any day but burn the snake with fire. From orbit. Slippery things with their fangs and venom and—GAH!

I caught up with the weirdest family in the world and kept my headlamp pointed at the ground, alert for even the slightest movement.

My attention was so rapt, I didn't even know they stopped walking until I blundered into Rick. He turned, holding a finger to his lips and tapping at his headlamp. His eyes were crazy wide, too. He turned his headlamp off. So did the other two. I followed suit.

Shit, apparently, was about to go down.

There was something very military about their movements and tactics. Close, but not quite. Regardless, I felt like I was back on Geru during the Gerunian Wars in my Skull Daggers days and infiltrating a bug nest before taking out the enemy's comms.

My heart thudded. I crouched a bit while my fellow hunters crept upright moving out of the tall grasses and further into the scrub.

If not for the moon, I would have been running blind.

They stopped, dropped to a knee. Side by side. I moved next to Ro and he handed me the elephant gun. I grinned. Time to fuck up some kangaroos and—

It happened so fast, I didn't have time to register the rustling in the tree above me.

All I knew was the growling and clawing, and sharp teeth buried into my shoulder. The other three stood. Someone, maybe Rick, muttered, "Fuckin' hell, get it off'im, Polly."

"He's fine," Paul said.

"Fuck you, Paul," I said and ripped whatever the hell was trying to kill me off. I threw it into the tree trunk.

It made a garbled snarl and scrambled at me.

The moonlight was just enough. I slammed the butt of the elephant gun down onto its head. The skull cracked. More like a thick pop. It didn't move. Pain laced through my shoulder, but, other than that, I was okay.

"The shit was that?" I asked, backing away from it.

"Drop bear, mate," Paul said and clapped me on the back. "Remember?" He grinned.

I shifted away from him. "Touch me again, Paul, and I'll bash your brains in too."

Oddly enough, the guy didn't respond. Instead, he returned his attention to the night before us.

"They're gone," he said after a long moment. "Drop bear attack alerted'em."

"What the shit is a drop bear?" I asked.

"A diseased form of koala," Ro said. "Like I told you."

"Well, isn't that just lovely," I said and turned back toward the Land Cruisers.

"Where the fuck you goin'?" Paul asked, sounding irritated as all hell.

He didn't like not being in control. I'd had to deal with his type many times. Only one way to get through.

"Back to the Land Cruiser, buttnugget. I think I know where your 'roos' are going." I turned my headlamp on. Because, snakes.

I smiled when I heard them all hurry to catch up to me.

"You don't know the bush, mate," Paul said. He turned his headlamp on and shined the damn thing at me. "Can't just go on without a guide."

"Then be my guide," I said as we entered the tall grasses. I kept my headlamp trained toward the ground.

"I…" He cleared his throat. "I'm a hunter. Not a guide."

"Look," I said. "I get it. You need to be in control. And you are. But I am trained to track and kill. Fifteen years of this shit. Let me do what I do best, and I think we'll be just fine."

Paul didn't say anything until we emerged from the tall grasses and approached the Land Cruisers.

"They migrated after the drop bear attack," Paul said. "Heading south."

"How do you know?"

He nodded in what I assumed was south. "Heard'em move in that direction just before you bashed that bear's head in, mate."

"Well, aren't you Mr. Observant?" I said, opened the door to my Land Cruiser, and placed the elephant gun in the backseat. "I'll follow you. But, don't stop so far away. Go another fifty yards."

He frowned. "They'll run."

"Thought these things were super aggressive?"

"They are," he said, "but bloody sensitive too. Loud noises, any real noises, they run or attack. Most of the time, they run."

Paul was falling into place, just as others had before him. The trick was to make them *think* they were still in control, though lead them in the right direction at the same time. A tactic I perfected over the years dealing with duh-heads like Paul. And maybe Paul wasn't such a duh-head after all. Maybe he realized who really needed to be pulling the strings.

It happened a lot. Some dudes just got off on the power-trip, when they shouldn't be in power at all. Knowing where and when to fool them was within the power of any individual willing to try.

Even so, Paul seemed genuine. Despite our little spats, he seemed to truly care about things and that's what drove him. He just didn't like losing control.

"Okay," I said. "Park where you want, but follow my lead after, understand?"

His jaw clenched and he glanced away for a moment. When his gaze returned to me, he sighed. "You're bloody impossible. But okay, we'll follow you."

Rick and Ro walked up to Paul. He shot them a glare, sighed again, and trudged to his vehicle.

Once he shut the door, Rick said, "He's never done that before."

"What?"

"Let some bloke tell'im what to do."

I chuckled. "Well, guess he just needed to meet the right bloke, eh?" I frowned. "I mean…never mind. Let's go."

Rick and Ro exchanged a smile. Rick hurried over to Paul's truck. Ro tried shooing me out of the driver's seat.

"Fuck off, Ol'Timer. My turn."

Ro shook his head. "Nah. Move your cunt ass over. I drive."

I crawled over into the passenger seat. "Okay, okay…don't have a stroke."

Ro keyed the ignition. "We don't get strokes in my family."

I flapped my arms in mock exasperation. "Fine. Don't break a hip. Whatever. Hey, Paul's leavin'."

Ro shook his head, put the Land Cruiser in gear and followed his son.

FIVE

"Park by the rocks," Paul said over the CB. "Don't fuck us up, Clusterfuk."

I snorted. "That kinda rhymed."

Ro sighed and parked. He got out without saying anything.

Guess I struck a nerve? I shrugged, grabbed the elephant gun, a couple handfuls of bullets and met with the family while they gathered near Paul's Land Cruiser.

I filled both side pockets of the vest with bullets and said, "We see'em, we kill'em. Simple. C'mon." I strode right by them, ignoring the burning glare from Paul. At least, I thought it was Paul. Ro was getting a bit on the testy side that night.

Soon enough, I heard them following.

Sometimes, all it took was someone who didn't give a fuck.

A few minutes passed and I crouched behind some scrub, headlamp off. The others crowded around me. Which made me want to cock punch each of them, but whatever. Hated being crowded. I was free to move when the time came.

Directly ahead, the jacked-up kangaroos were tearing a crocodile to ribbons. Not far, I heard the silvery flow of a river just below the growls and ripping of tough flesh from the kangaroos.

There were eight of the bastards. All of them feasting on the croc.

"Spread out," I whispered. "Make a U-shape. When I whistle, kill the bastards."

None of them said anything. Not even Paul. They moved away, keeping low and, shit, I almost teared up. They were amateurs, but well-balanced amateurs. I was witnessing a family business in action. Or something. Anyway, it was fucking beautiful.

The moonlight gave away their positions. Only Ro crouched a little too far away, but the plan should work. Each one aimed their elephant guns at the group of rabid roos.

Roos?

GAH!

KANGAroos.

Stupid Aussie slang being addictive and shit.

I aimed my own gun directly at the back of the largest kangaroo and whistled.

The night exploded like thunder and four of the creatures dropped dead. Blood still misted the night air when the other four squealed and spun away from the croc.

"Jesus fell off the cross," I muttered, noting the long teeth glinting in the pale light. The foam glopping from their open, shrieking mouths.

But it was their amber eyes that stopped me. They weren't rabid. Something else was going on. Something much deeper than some mutated, earthly disease.

"Fire," I roared and squeezed the trigger.

The one I aimed at, its head turned to crimson splatter. The other three dropped, collapsing over each other in a gory fashion.

I reloaded the elephant gun and stood from the scrub.

Rick and Ro whooped at the victory. Paul, he gave me a nod. I didn't nod back and pointed at the amber eyes glowing in the direction of the river. He did that double-take thing and looked at me all wide-eyed.

I gave him a thumbs up and ran into the small clearing where the creatures were feeding, leaped over a corpse, and skidded to a stop in front of three sets of eyes. They growled. A deep rumble. I leveled my gun on the right-side set of eyes, trigger nearly squeezed when something heavy crashed into me. The gun flew from my hands and went rolling into a nearby tree. Pain surged through me from what seemed to be everywhere.

A growl snapped my attention away from the pain seconds before the beast came at me again.

I rolled away and the rabid thing bashed itself against the tree trunk. It didn't stop doing that until I gained my feet and swung the .30-.60 rifle slung across my back, around. Bloodied, lower jaw flapping, it pounced at me. I fired three shots into its head before it barely left the ground. All it managed was a slight hop before falling to the side, blood oozing from its head.

Close up, they were terrifying. Big teeth and amber eyes, sure. But what was with the torn, rotten hide that hung from their faces? They weren't zombies, just horrifically diseased kangaroos, but damn…they were messed up. And…since when did kangaroos have big, pointy teeth? Something wasn't right. Diseased or not, they were mutated and decaying at the same time.

No matter how fucked up the strain of rabies the guys thought it was, it shouldn't mutate the animals.

Or would it?

Shit, I didn't know. I wasn't a goddamn scientist.

All I knew, my gut told me something rotten hopped through the outback. Like putrid rotten. A dead carp turning to soup in the hot summer sun kind of putrid.

I took out the lurking roos and motioned for the guys to join me.

"Good work, mate," Rick said. All smiles, that guy.

Ro nodded while he looked at all the dead roos.

Paul, though, he shook his head. "You're a reckless wanker."

I blinked. "Did you…did you just call me a wanker?"

"Yep," Paul said and pointed at the roo that bum-rushed me. "That one 'bout tore your fucking head off, mate."

"Go wank your wanker, ya wanker spankin' redneck."

Everyone fell silent. Rick and Ro glanced at each other, faces slackening in the glow of our headlamps. Paul gaped at me, hands curling into fists at his sides. I recognized the look in his eyes. Saw it many times over the years.

I swung the .30-.60 around so it hung at my back. Just in case. "What?" I moved closer to Paul.

He didn't move. Didn't flinch. Didn't blink. Even though I was a good six inches taller than him and broader built, Paul stood his ground. Not that I wanted a fight. Okay, maybe I did. Shit was getting boring in Australia and I needed…*something*. A fist fight with Paul, though, that would last only a couple of seconds. Then what? I'd be bored all over again.

Sigh.

Slowly, the corners of Paul's cheeks puffed out. His eyes squinted. His body shook. A weird noise whined in his throat.

I backed away a step. "Uh…you gonna explode dude? Because, the guy who exploded all over me…it wasn't good." I frowned. "Wait, that came out wrong." I blew out a sigh. Came? "Damn it!"

That's when Paul burst out laughing. Like, full out donkey bray laughter that echoed through the entire fucking outback. Behind him, Rick and Ro chuckled, though I could tell they were just as confused as I was.

Paul staggered forward, patted my shoulders and managed, between laughter, "You're a good bloke." More laughter, finally winding down to chuckles. Tears streamed his leathery cheeks. He turned and walked away. "Let's get a schooner."

"What the actual shit is a schooner?" I asked.

"We need to burn'em, Polly," Rick said, totally avoiding my question. Because he was a dickweasel like that. Not really.

Paul waved a hand. "So, burn'em. I'll be in the Land Cruiser." He disappeared through the brush, still chuckling.

I turned to Rick and Ro, an eyebrow raised. They both gave me identical shrugs and went about tossing the dead roos in a pile. I threw a few on the pile myself. They doused everything with gasoline.

Before they set the pile of dead things on fire I said, "Hold up a sec."

I crouched, carefully inspecting one of the creatures. When I didn't find anything I could really get behind, nearly threadlike tentacles slithered out of the kangaroo's ear. Dozens of blue threads. I stepped away, eyes widening.

"What is it?" Rick asked.

"Parasites," I muttered. "Alien."

"What—"

"Burn'em," I shouted. "Now, before they crawl out of the bodies!"

Rick jerked, as though slapped, struck a match and tossed it on the corpses. The entire pile burst into flames.

I kept my attention on the blue thread-like tendrils slithering out of the ear. And not just that ear. A few more sported their own tendrils. And, just as the fire blazed over all the corpses, I caught a glimpse of what was living inside the kangaroos. It wriggled out, a lizard-like creature. Thousands of blue tendrils lashed at the air, immediately disappearing into the flames. The parasite itself squealed before it was fully consumed by the fire.

The reek of burned hair mixed with the savory aroma of cooking meat. The stench was so cloying, I wanted to both vomit and eat something.

More squeals floated out of the fires. Very brief, but there.

I rounded the burning pile to join Rick and Ro.

"What did you mean by parasite?" Ro asked.

"It's not rabies," I said. "The kangaroos are being mutated and controlled by alien parasites. I don't know what species of parasites, but I've seen it before."

Rick blinked at me. "You have?"

I grunted. "A few times. Fire kills just about anything. You've been settin' them on fire from the beginning?"

Both Rick and Ro nodded.

"Well, that's fabulous," I said. "We just leave this to burn here, or can we leave?"

Ro gave the area a quick gander. "Nothin' here to really catch. We got them soaked with gas before lighting. They'll be ash by mornin'."

"So," I said, "we're not gonna start a bush fire, or whatever?"

Ro smiled. "Probably be for the best if there was, but no."

I dug his reasoning, but, yeah. Time to get out of there.

We trudged back to the Land Cruisers.

Not long after, I found myself at a small pub scattered with assholes. Well, more or less. Like all bars, there were a few good drunks scattered about. I happened to be with three good ones at the bar. I slugged down a "schooner" in no more than a minute. Which, I guess, was impressive. If I didn't have respect from my newfound team before, I did then. Paul was an obnoxious weirdo when dunk, but at least he was delightful weird too.

He sang every song the speakers spouted, especially a classic tune by AC/DC. He didn't calm down and sing nicely until the lyrics for the Cold Chisel song, "When the War is Over", flowed through the raucous laughter and loud chats. He sat beside me, upended a shot of whiskey and turned to me.

"You did," Paul lit a cigarette, "what I couldn't do, mate." He drew in a puff and blew out a jet of silvery smoke.

The smell instantly made me want one, but I soon shoved the impulse away. I quit smoking a couple years ago. No matter what they said, that craving never really went away.

"What did I do?" I asked.

Paul snorted, grabbed his schooner and drank. When he finished, he said, "Killed twenty of'em all in one blow. You said they're not rabid. Controlled by parasites. You win, ya wanker."

I laughed and partied with them, though I found myself thinking about the roos and the alien parasites. Where the shit did the parasites come from? What species? Were they planted on Earth millions of years ago and finally spread when the climate went to shit? Or did some alien assholes make a drive-by parasite drop on a few countries?

For the first time in a long time, I couldn't really kick back, drink and shoot the shit. I frowned at all the bottles behind the bar, mind churning. Something fucked up was going on. A subtle invasion? That felt like the most likely.

"Fuckin' emus," Ro muttered from behind. I turned on my stool to find the old man with a schooner of beer in one hand and snapping a salute with the other.

"Rick, Paul?" I said over the chattering crowd. "I think your dad just fell off the diving board in the shallow end."

Rick nudged me. "Nah. True story, those emus."

"Agile buggers, emus," Paul said. "Fuckin' hell. Ya gotta see'em to know."

"1905," Ro said, voice booming over the chatter. "Those cunts were out of control. Fuckin' emus everywhere. Famers couldn't stop'em. They were shit shots, ya know? Government called in the military and those bastards wasted so many bullets on the birds until they finally just gave up." Ro lowered his head. "Australia's Greatest Defeat." He took a deep swig from his schooner.

I laughed, though almost everyone in the pub lowered their heads and drank.

"And," I said, "I feel like an idiot. This was a serious thing?"

"Over population means the birds eat everything, even crops," Rick said. "They were putting a hardship on our farmers back then."

I chuckled. "Wait, you guys went to war with Big Brid?"

"Better than with each other, mate," Paul spouted and yanked my schooner from my hand. He slammed his and mine on the bar. "Fill'em, dear."

The woman behind the bar shook her head, though filled our glass schooners without comment. Glass, Rick explained to me after my first drink (which was like six before that recent refill), was reserved for hunters and men and women who fought to keep Australia safe. Otherwise, it was aluminum mugs for everyone else.

So, I guess we were like the guests of honor at the little pub. Ah well, at least I didn't have to pay, heh. Take that, fuckers.

I agreed with Paul to some extent. "How did you all overcome the plight of emus?" I meant it to sound sarcastic, but Rick took it seriously. Because, of course he did.

"They were too agile and fast. Even the military couldn't stop'em." Rick sighed. "Sounds ridiculous now, but back then, they didn't have firepower. Low caliber rifles, machineguns and before those, a few flintlocks."

I blinked. "Y'all have some serious issues with the wildlife since forever, then? Damn..."

"Wasn't any flintlocks durin' The Great Emu War," Ro grumbled.

Paul handed me a cigarette, his own smoldering away between the first and second fingers of his right hand. The silvery smoke curled upward, joining the heavy cloud above us. I stared at the cigarette for a long time. I thought about putting it in my mouth, I imagined the lighter flickering into flame. That first, long inhale. The equally long exhale of smoke. The false sensation that all was going to be okay.

I snapped the cigarette in two and let the halves fall to the grimy floor.

"Fuckin' American wanker," Paul shot off his stool. "That durry cost more than your life!"

I stood. "Okay, I don't know what the shit a durry is, but I don't want a cigarette."

Paul rushed me. I sidestepped and he crashed into the bar.

"Should have just put the durry in your pocket, mate," Rick said. "Polly doesn't give'em out like that to just anyone. Means he respects you." Rick sighed. "Well, he used to."

"I don't just put any durry in my pocket, Rick. I'm not a—"

Paul charged at me again. I sidestepped again. He stumbled into a table of rugged looking dudes who might not have showered since the Ming Dynasty. They blasted Paul with all kinds of Aussie obscenities. Or, at least I thought they were obscenities. Aussies were so weird with their insults.

Before I knew it, one of the big men held Paul while the other slammed giant fists into the guy's stomach.

I sighed and tapped the punching dude on his filthy shoulder. He spun, teeth gritted.

"*Holy* shit," I said. "You are one ugly motherfucker. Just had to come see for myself. My eyesight isn't what it used to be and—"

He threw a big, sloppy, haymaker. I caught his fist, twisted his arm so hard the elbow popped. The guy howled, knees giving up. He dropped to the floor and I slammed a knee into his face. Blood and teeth flew through the air.

"Fucker," the guy who was holding Paul bellowed. He tossed Paul aside and came at me like a goddamn grizzly bear. Arms up, mouth open.

I punched the bastard square in the face. I felt his nose break under my knuckles. He dropped beside his brother, or friend, probably lover, howling in pain. Blood leaking from between his thick fingers.

I helped Paul to his feet and led him to the bar. I gave the bartender a nod and, oddly enough, she knew exactly what I meant. Maybe not so odd. I bet she had to deal with a lot of shitstorms in the little hole in the wall pub. She placed a fresh schooner of beer in front of Paul. He made a jagged chuckle, lifted the schooner, then drank about half of it in one go.

"Better leave, mate," the bartender said. "Those two are mercs."

I snorted. "Mercs? Jumping Jesus flippin' out an airplane, seriously?"

She nodded, though appeared a bit bewildered.

I got that a lot.

"If they're mercs, I'm the—"

"Look out!" She ducked behind the bar.

I turned just in time to earn a bullet to the gut. The force of it slammed me into the bar. A .357? Really? Leave it to burly assholes to pick a .357. The pain, as always, was nearly crippling. Yet, I stormed toward the man. He blinked, fired another shot before I twisted the gun out of his hand, slammed the muzzle to his forehead, I pulled the trigger. Whatever brains the bastard had ended oozing down the wall behind him. I shoved him aside and pointed the pistol at his brother, or whatever. The one still on the floor missing teeth from my knee.

He held up trembling arms, face twisted in a sob. Tears and blood slathered his dirty face.

"Drag your lover outta here and never come back," I said through the shooting pains in my stomach.

The dude nodded. It took him a bit, but he managed to pull his partner out of the pub.

I turned, slammed the pistol on the bar. "Next time assholes start shit, use that," I told the bartender. "Don't even have to shoot'em. A warning shot should be enough."

She blinked at me, nodded, and slipped the gun under the bar.

"Ya got any Jameson?" I asked.

She smiled. "Yep."

"Fan-fucking-tastic. Gimme a triple."

"You're hurt," Rick said. "He shot you twice."

I waved him away. "I'll be alright. How's Paul?"

Rick tapped my shoulder and pointed across the pub to a small booth where Paul was being "mended" by two women. He noticed us looking and grinned.

I chuckled. "I like him better already."

"You should be dying," Ro said, his bushy eyebrows knitting in a frown.

"Oh," I said. "Right. This is what happens when alien blood soaks into you. My body heals itself. Slow as hell, but I'll be the same Clusterfuk y'all know and love by morning."

I didn't watch their reactions. Instead, I focused my attention on the bartender. "What's your name, hun?"

She smiled, kind of backed away. Trying to play hard to get and failing. "Willie."

"Willie," I said, or more like shouted over the music blasting from the speakers. I winked at her. "What are you doing after work?"

She smiled.

A couple of hours later, the pub empty, I bent Willie over the bar and gave her the full Clusterfuk.

To my surprise, she turned out to be a clinger instead of a runner.

Shit.

"Do you have to go?" She asked, stroking me. "We could do this every night."

"The guys need me, hun," I said, moving away from her and getting into my clothes before she could grapple on again. "Lot of them parasitic roos hoppin' around, ya know."

"Tomorrow night, then?" She pressed her naked body up against me, lips nibbling on my neck.

I almost caved and gave it to her again. Almost.

I stepped back, chuckling. "Maybe. See ya later, hun."

The holes in my stomach were still leaking blood, though nothing alarming. The healing thing still did its job, thank the gods of grape jelly. The pain was still there, though nothing sharp or paralyzing. By morning the holes would be gone.

As happened during such times, the past flickered through my mind.

The scrawny creature that broke into our home. The alien monster. The thing that tore my mother and father apart before I could kill it. And the blood. All that blood splashing onto me and soaking through my skin. The searing pain as its blood merged with mine. The time some disgruntled old man stabbed me when I was seventeen and didn't die. A few hours, I was healed. Not even a mark where the bastard stabbed me.

I would probably die. But I could also heal myself. Slowly, but still…not many folks could say their bodies naturally healed.

It was weird, and yet, made me who I was.

I blamed the Skull Daggers for my enhanced strength and speed, though. Those assholes injected me with so much shit…

Ro, Rick and Paul were all asleep in the Land Cruisers when I strolled up.

I sighed and leaned against one of the vehicles. My mind drifted to Paul's cigarettes. Durrys. Whatever. Smoking wouldn't kill me, of course. My lungs would heal the next day. For me, even though I enjoyed smoking, one needed to put aside childish addictions and grow.

And…that sounded way too philosophical. Who was I, even? Gah. I blamed Australia…

Okay, it was more like, they didn't have cigarettes up in space often. And if they did, the cigs were weird alien concoctions that tasted funky and left me all weird for a few hours. I didn't quit to be healthy. I quit because it just didn't compare to beating someone's brains in. Especially the bugs. Millions upon millions of alien species of bugs everywhere. Some were even intelligent enough to outsmart an army of men, vicious, yet they were trapped in collective thought and sensation most of the time. Which, in the end, worked perfectly to dive in and just blast'em to fuckin' bloody bits.

The frogs and crickets did their nightly orchestra thing. Reminded me of late summer nights in Iowa. Even the sweat trickling down my butt crack. Ah…good times.

Eventually, I walked back to the pub where Willie was picking up a few stray bottles and schooners.

She frowned. "Forget something, mate?"

I shook my head, closed the door, and took her to Clusterfuk town again. Because, why not?

42

SIX

All told, I spent two years in Australia (that's Straya to you, ya bloody cunt).

Longest two years of my fuckin' life.

Still, I settled in. Not like I could be beamed up by Admiral Goat Fucker or anything. I figured I was going to die in the land of schooners and g'day's and bloody cunts.

It wasn't all bad though. Especially when I started up my side business. It was a year after joining the family of roo murderers. They felt like…family…

"Yup," Paul told me when I laid it out for him. "That's still illegal, mate."

"Yeah, but…think about how all the money could help your roo business."

"Government pays good enough," Paul said. "I'm not gettin' into anything bloody illegal and ruining that."

I snorted and swept a hand at the large, but very ramshackle house we all shared. "Right. I mean, look at that mansion we all live in. From the golden showers to the leopard skin bedsheets. Such a wonderful shithole it is!"

"It shelters us." Paul placed an elephant gun in the back of the Land Cruiser. "That's all we need."

I spit out my gum in a bout of laughter. When it eased, I said, "Dude, last night my bed was turned into a goddamn waterbed. Literally. Like, I was soaked. Why? Because there's a fuckin' hole the shape of Minnesota in the ceiling."

He shrugged, slammed the hatch shut. "So, patch it. Aren't all you Yank blokes into that sort of shit?"

I gasped. "That's racist!"

Paul shook his head and started toward the driver's side. "Do what you want, mate. Leave me'n my family out of it, right?"

He climbed into the Land Cruiser before I could reply, the cockdrizzling bastard.

That was the day I parted ways with the small family who hunted parasite infested roos and set out on my own.

Because, you can't spell dumb without the d.

Wait…

Anyway, I stole one of their vehicles, an elephant gun, pistol, .30-.60, and a machete and some food. And boxes of ammo. And some bottled water. And a heavy-duty tent. And I hooked a boat up to the

Land Cruiser. And a box of matches. And blankets and pillows, because, damn it, I needed my beauty rest.

I almost left the boat. Almost. But, ya know…I kinda needed it too.

They'd understand.

And, from that day forward, I became: Crocodile Clusterfuk.

First few days were rough, living out in the bush with all the creepy killing machines running about, but, eventually, I showed them all who their daddy was.

That's right, I became one with fuckin' nature.

Not really. I just killed every goddamn thing that got too close. Even ants. Scuttling little bastards…

In a month, though, I was banking, bro. Like, thousands of dollars a week.

I was near the end of my second year in Australia when they fucked everything up.

"You have two choices," a man shouted from the bank. "Come ashore, or we report you to the Australian Government for poaching."

I pulled the croc onto the boat and squinted toward shore. Six men, from what I could tell. All standing no more than a foot from the water. Three arrow shaped ripples appeared about twenty feet from where the men stood.

It hadn't taken me long after starting up the business to know what those ripples meant.

I waved at them. "Get the fuck away from the bank!"

"Clint Clusterfuk," the main man, and closest to the water, shouted. "Come ashore now, or we will report you."

"Dude," I shouted back. "The shit you talkin' about? Get away from the fuckin' water! There's—"

"You have exactly one minute to comply."

The water arrowheads were only about six feet away.

"Seriously," I shouted. "Back up! You're too close to the water!"

The ripples stopped about two feet away.

I lifted the elephant rifle and aimed at the closest ripple before it stopped. "Get the fuck back," I shouted. "You're—"

All six men in suits drew sidearms and pointed them in my direction, the dum-nuts. Note: Not bum-nuts, but dum-nuts. Because, authenticity, and shit.

I opened my mouth to yell at them again, when the massive jaws burst out of the water. I drew a quick bead and squeezed the trigger.

Boom.

Literally, it was like thunder.

The croc's head exploded in shards of bone and ribbons of red. The other two crocs thrashed and jetted away. On the shore, the man in charge stumbled backward, tripped and fell flat on his ass.

"Assholes," I said and started the boat motor.

It took no time for the aluminum boat to scratch the sandy bottom. I stepped over two dead crocs, pulled the boat up onto shore and spun on the idiots.

"Are you dumb?" I asked. "Because, that's how you get dumb." I pointed the elephant gun at the guy on the ground. "Dumbass."

The other five closed in, pistols on me. Okay, so they were at least trained. Maybe not dumb at all, except for being in the Australian bush and near its rivers. And that, I could forgive. A little.

The dude on the ground stood, dusted himself off. He was shaking, and for good reason. The guy would've been croc food if not for me. Still, the asshole in him made him swagger toward me. He held a thin, though irritated grin on his thin face. His white, bald head glimmered with sweat in the hot Aussie sun.

"Who the fuck *are* you?" I kept him at rifle length. Whoever he and his team were, I didn't trust them. At all.

Maybe I should've let the crocs eat'em…

The bald dude straightened out his black suit. "We are here to bring you to Xenia."

It took a moment for me to remember the name. But only a moment. Xenia was what the Intergalactic Council were thinking about naming Earth Two before I was sent to Australia.

I grunted. "Yeah?" I brushed by the man and his small team to my camp where a large croc hung, its blood partially filling a large hole under it.

My clients wanted croc jerky and the hides. I tried to provide both. And that one was due for butchering. I brought out a Bowie knife I bought a couple months ago and slit the croc from lower jaw to the tip of its tail.

The men surrounded me while I worked.

"You are," the dude said, "Clint Clusterfuk, correct?"

"Depends," I said and began peeling the croc's hide downward from its tail. "Who are you, and what the shit do you want?"

"Your former employers said you'd be poaching crocodiles," the bald man said. "You're the only man we've spotted doing so."

I chuckled. "Poaching? You're adorable. I have legit business goin' on here."

"According to Australian law, the killing of croc—"

"Pump the hate brakes, baldy. What the hell do you want?" I turned to face him, croc blood dripping from my hands.

He gave me a withering look. "For your cooperation."

"Yeah, well, as you can see…I'm pretty busy, so…"

"Our employer wishes to speak with you, Mr. Clusterfuk." He paused. "What kind of a name is Clusterfuk, anyway?"

I stabbed the Bowie knife into the croc's belly and made a long cut all the way down to the animal's throat. I shrugged. "It's Norwegian."

Mr. Baldy made a slight gagging sound. "Well, we are required to bring you to our employer for further briefing. You come highly recommended by Admiral Burlow."

I scooped the croc's guts out and let them splat on the ground at my boots. Old boots. Learned my lesson with the first gutting. Jesus Sloppy Ass Mess, I had looked like I just stepped out of a slaughterhouse blood vat. Okay, not really, but it got my jeans and boots all fucked up and stinky. I made those my work boots. The good ones were in the tent. They made good pub hoppers and just going on a walkabout.

Psst. That means walking around a lot and looking at shit, for you American cunts.

"Highly recommended, eh?" I kicked the guts into a prepared hole and went about slicing around the feet.

"Y-Yes, he—listen, do you really have to do that right now?"

I stopped, shot him a glance. "Look. Every minute this river dick with teeth is exposed to the heat, the worse the meat gets. Like chicken, and shit. Whatever. You get the picture. So, keep talkin'. I haven't killed ya yet, have I?" I made a twirling "go ahead" gesture with my knife.

"He thinks he's Crocodile Dundee," one of the men near Baldy whispered.

I spun, flinging blood off my knife at the men. They all jumped and stumbled away like it was acid or something. Pussies.

I narrowed my gaze at the man who whispered. He was taller than Baldy, broader, with a dusting of black hair on top. His brown eyes widened when he noticed me glaring at him.

"Guuurl," I said and moved toward him, knife dripping blood when I pointed it at him. "I'm Crocodile Clusterfuk. If you ever so much as whimper the entire time you're here, I swear to the fuckin' gods, I'll gut you just like this ol' croc. Got me?"

For a second, he actually appeared scared, which was what I was going for. But then…

He burst out laughing. Like full out, doubled over, gut punch, donkey bray laughter.

Well, that's a new one. No one ever laughed at me like that before. It actually gave me pause, the bastard. The others stepped away from the laughing man.

Heh, guess some of them are smart.

I stormed to the laughing man, kneed him in his braying face, grabbed his throat and hauled him off his feet. The laughter cut off in a squeak. Nose broken, blood drained out over his quivering mouth. He was about as tall as me, so I didn't keep him held up for long before slamming the bastard down hard onto the ground. All the air exploded out his lungs and he rolled around in the dirt gasping and gagging.

I kneeled beside him and placed the bloody blade of the Bowie knife against his throat. "I've killed men for less." I leaned in close to his ear. "Remember that."

I stood, gave Baldy a glare and returned to the hanging croc. "Get on with it, asshat."

Carefully, I peeled the hide from the feet. It was intricate work, despite what people would think. Collectors wanted the whole hide. Fully intact. In that business, it was the collectors and weird foodies you needed to appease. At two grand per hide and another grand for the meat…damn right I was going to appease them.

When Baldy didn't say anything, I blew out my cheeks in a heavy breath. "C'mon dude. Why was I highly recommended? Because, last I knew I was exiled."

I peeled the tail hide away. With the feet free, it was go time. With a massive yank downward, I managed to pull everything to the head free of the carcass.

"Uh," Baldy said, sounding all choked up. Not because he was going to cry, but because he was about to puke. "The Admiral said you were the best soldier ever placed under his command."

I chuckled, slicing around the croc's massive jaws. "That lyin' bastard. What else he tell ya?"

"Only where you were exiled. We met with your former colleagues and eventually figured out where you might be."

"They're all a bunch'o cunts, mate," Paul said, stepping through some scrub.

I stopped, blinked. "God…you're even uglier with a beard."

Paul snorted. "At least I can grow one."

"Hey, now." I lifted the Bowie knife. "I shave, asshole. It's what responsible adults do."

He waved a dismissive hand. "I see you're still a bloody cunt."

I winked and turned back to the croc. "The bloodiest." I made a few more cuts. "How much they pay you?"

"Enough," Paul said. "If you hadn't gone on and done this, I would've lied."

"You fuckin' liar," I said, carefully wriggling the jaw and head hide from the body. "You would've given me up anyway just to save your own ass. Even though your ass didn't need saving."

"Well," Paul said, "if you'd stayed with us…"

"Oh, shut up. You would've done the same." I returned my attention to Baldy. "If you take me…" I patted Paul's shoulder, "you're takin' this lanky wanker with too."

Baldy's eyes narrowed a bit.

"The fuck you on about?" Paul spouted. He backed away from me and the suits. "I'm not goin' nowhere." He drew a forty-five and pointed it at Baldy.

"Sir," Baldy said. "We only have orders to retrieve, Mr. Clusterfuk. I assure you we won't—"

"Oh, nonsense pumpdump," I said and snatched the pistol from Paul's hand. "Polly here can hunt down a flea in a swamp. I mean, look at him." I made a gesture akin to a gameshow girl. "It's a *new* Aussie! Sure, he looks a bit rough 'round the edges, but he's a family man with an awful temper who pissed into the wind once, and only once. Because, *this* man cannot be fooled twice!"

Paul backed away from me some more. "You've fuckin' cracked, mate."

I tossed the pistol at his feet, grinned. "Like a goddamn hardboiled egg." I put the full glower on. Staring him down and inching closer. My hands curled into fists. I puffed my chest out a bit. Paul withered, though not as much I had hoped.

I loomed over him.

His eyes widened.

I lifted a fist and he cowered. "Look, mate, I don't mean nothin' by it. I just don't wanna go to fuckin' space."

My fist trembled above my head. I made my face into one of pure rage. Veins popped out on my neck. Pretty sure my face turned all red too.

I brought the fist down fast and—

I stopped an inch from Paul's shoulder and smiled. "Just kidding, cuntnugget. You need to be here to stop the roo invasion."

He let go a heavy breath, nearly collapsed, then wiped sweat from his leathery forehead. "You're a fuckin' cunt, mate," he said, chuckled and picked the pistol up off the ground. He holstered it.

"When I come back here," I said, "I want all those parasitic roos dead and burned to ashes. Ya bloody wanker sniffer."

Paul shook his head. "It's only us now. I don't think—"

"Oh, for fuck sake, Paul. Just say yes. You're gettin' all dramatic on me."

He smiled. "Yeah. They'll be dead, mate."

"Fantastic!" I planted a kiss on his tanned, leathery cheek and whispered in his ear. "You taste like beef jerky."

He shoved me back, shaking his head. "Get outta here, ya cunt." His smile resurfaced.

"That better mean I'm a good cunt, because I don't know if I could handle being a bad cunt. I already feel dirty..."

Paul snorted. "Good one. See you 'round?"

Aw, that struck the feels pretty hard. I kinda stammered a bit, though finally said, "Yeah, mate. Some day. You take care of this place, okay?"

He gave me a firm nod.

"Gah," I said and opened my arms. "Bring it in, brother."

He frowned.

"Come on. It's right here. Come get all up in this Clusterfuk. Ya know you want it."

Paul shuddered. "Nah, mate. But you take care."

I let my arms fall to my sides. "Well, that's just rude." I turned away. "Be gone, Jerky Man."

"Thank you for—"

"I SAID BE GONE."

I listened to him chuckle and walk away before facing Baldy. He appeared to be on the ninth level of confused.

"Ready?"

Baldy lifted a dark eyebrow. "What about that...thing?" He pointed to the partially processed croc.

I shrugged. "Probably best we go soon. The Aussie DNR are pretty strict about poaching crocodiles." I made a jerking off gesture. "Not like they don't have a gazillion of the snapping fuckers swimming in the rivers, am I right?"

Baldy didn't know what to say, that silly bastard.

"Uh, you ready?" I asked.

He laughed, a bit nervously, then appeared to snap out of it. He straightened out his uniform, cleared his throat, and said, "Yes. This way."

Funny thing was, I didn't go full Clusterfuk. Then again, I rarely went full Clusterfuk unless I had to.

It was a gift.

SEVEN

"You need to cryo-sleep," the little bastard told me.

He wasn't human, nor alien, though I suspected android.

"No worries. I'll hang out until we get there."

"Our destination is approximately one thousand, two hundred lightyears away," the little fucker said. "If you are not in cryo-sleep, you will not survive the journey."

I was just messing with it, of course. Cryo-sleep was imperative to intergalactic travel.

"Fine," I said and stepped into the cryo-sleep pod. "But I'm not gonna be happy about it, jacknuts."

"Very fine, sir," the android man thing said. "Once the pod is sealed, count backward from five."

Before I could protest, the pod door slipped shut, sealing me in. A whoosh of cold air engulfed me.

I didn't even get to three when everything blinked out of existence.

***

Waking up after cryo-sleep was supposed to be slow. It needed to be. If a person was shaken awake before their allotted time, they went bonkers.

Apparently, someone forgot to mention that to my current handlers because...

"Up and at'em, Clusterfuk," a man boomed into my ear, followed by a sharp crack to the right side of my face.

Did the fucknut really just slap me?

Regardless, I was too out of it to break his hand off and shove it up his ass. All I saw were blurry, gray shapes like moving water in front of me. A big one, my slap happy jerkfuck, I assumed, and a smaller one.

"Jesus, Wayne," a softer voice said. "You can't wake them up like that. They—"

"Well, you sure as hell don't know who this big bastard is, do you?"

"Well, not personally, but—"

"It's fuckin' Clint Clusterfuk. Dude was a hero before he crossed the line. Heard he took out his entire platoon during a rage."

What…the…shit? So, that's what everyone thought happened? That I simply went nuttybars and killed everyone? And that whole hero thing needed to go too. A hero, I was not. At all.

And, speaking of rage…it burned hot now. Liquid fire surged, clearing my vision and waking my body up. I didn't even wait for the tingling to stop.

"Hey," the smaller man said and pointed at me. "I think he's—"

I bashed my knuckles into the side of the bigger guy's face. He snapped a shocked expression at me, then his eyes rolled up revealing only the whites. He swayed a second or two, then toppled over.

I stepped out of the cryo-pod and over the assnugget, towering over the smaller man. He didn't back down or cower though, so he got a couple bonus points there. But damn he was ugly. Like Frankenstein's Monster ugly. Only born that way. I blamed Maybelline.

"Mr. Clusterfuk," the guy said and smiled. "Your meeting with Rune is in half an hour. Your retrievers said you should, perhaps, freshen up a bit before your meeting."

I sniffed my armpit, cringed, grunted. "Bastards. I smell fabulous."

"Your shower has already been scheduled," the small man said and turned away. He hurried to a set of metal doors. "I'm Mr. Scott, and I'll be your guide during your time here on Blu."

I followed him. "Blu? Never heard of her."

"Not many have," Scott said. The door slid open and he grinned over his shoulder. "My employer likes to be a ghost." He hurried on down a narrow white hall.

The brightness of it about gave me a seizure. They really needed to get their shit together with whole cryo-sleep thing. All that brightness wasn't good either. Two things I survived upon waking. I blamed my healing factor. My alien blood mixture, whatever. That shit puts a halt to a lot of things. I probably should have been dead a thousand times over by now.

Meh. Sometimes you got used to being kinda immortal.

Either that, or you went wonky.

I wasn't wonky. At least I don't think I was wonky? Why didn't I have any friends…?

Shit.

Mr. Scott was like a goddamn bullet, as fast as he was walking. For such a small dude, he was a speedy bastard.

"Who's your employer?" I asked.

"You'll meet him soon enough. First thing's first, however." He stopped at another set of metal doors. They beeped and whispered open. "We need to get you cleaned up and in proper gear."

Ah. So, they were at least meta military here. Some structure. Similar phrases and words. Not that it mattered, but…

Wait, did I just join a militia without knowing?

Son of a bitch.

Guess I'd been through worse in the past, but a militia? Really? Militias are for old, fat, wannabes. Mostly a bunch of rando gun enthusiasts who didn't know as much about military training as they thought when it came to a real battle.

Still…I was in a motherfuckin' militia!

Spending so much time in Australia, I almost shouted, "Fuck ya, ya bloody cunts!" Almost.

The next hall was wider and mellower with gray, painted walls and white tiled floor. It eased my anxiety a bit and my body chilled the hell out for a few seconds.

"We have a room for you," Scott said. "Shower and gear will be ready."

"Uh-huh. Better be a woman in there too."

Mr. Scott snorted. "No women. You have approximately fifteen minutes to clean up and be ready to meet my employer."

"You've never been laid, have you?"

Scott, the little bastard, didn't reply. Instead, he powered forward until he came to a door on the right. He glanced at the black orb above the door and it slid open.

He turned to me and gestured toward the doorway. "See you in fifteen minutes."

I entered the room and the door slipped shut behind me. The lights flickered on. I sighed. On the bed were neatly folded black clothes. My gear. I gathered it up and went to the bathroom, which was little more than a closet. And, for a bigger dude like me, that shit was nuts. I swear I banged my head on the curtain rod more than once. Okay, not really. There wasn't a shower curtain. It had a glass door and all that shit.

But before I took a shower, certain matters needed attending. Cryo-sleep messed the body up. And even I wasn't immune to it. So, like clockwork, my bowels began to scream. Thank the gods there was a toilet.

Once all was said and done, I stepped out of the bathroom to find Mr. Scott standing there. He sported a weird little smirk on his face I didn't like. I kind of wanted to punch him, to be honest. A smug look on his face that just screamed for a fist to break it.

I didn't, though.

Give me that much credit, at least.

"You're running late," Scott said.

I walked over to the bed, towel tied around my hips, and checked out the clothing situation.

"My employer will not tolerate tardiness."

"Yeah, well," I said and let my towel drop. "Your eyebrows are too bushy."

"Mr. Clusterfuk," Scott said, sounding more than a little terrified. "There is a bathroom for you to dress in. I don't want to—"

I swung around, my full Clusterfuk swinging with me. "But Scotty! I love you!"

The look of pure horror gave me more pleasure than little Willie back in Aussie Land. Mmm, Willie…

Mr. Scott made a funny yip once he noticed I was getting hard and bolted for the door. Once he stumbled out of the room and the door shut, I chuckled.

"Silly bastard."

I got dressed.

Little Scotty stood in the hall, face all pale, eyes everywhere but on me.

"Sorry about the peep show, lil' fella," I said and clapped him on the back. "Let's go see this employer of yours."

He shivered and led the way.

EIGHT

I imagined Lil' Scotty's employer holed up in a massive room. Something like Admiral Burlow and his merry band of elderly people who sentenced me to Australia. Instead, a small door whispered open, giving way to modest living quarters.

Ah, Straya. I actually missed it. Funny, I wanted so badly to return to space and kill something, and yet I saw myself spending the rest of my life as an imposter Aussie. Scary as shit with all the snakes and spiders and crocs and parasitic roos, but…gods…it was beautiful too.

Sigh.

A black man, maybe in his late forties, greeted Mr. Scott and I at the door.

Lil' Scotty bowed a bit. "Your Honor, I apologize for our tardiness. Here is Mr. Clusterfuk, as requested."

The Honor guy, he rolled his eyes. "Scott. Go away."

The small dude flinched, turned, bumped into me, muttered something and ran out of the room. The door closed and I stood alone with the employer. The Honor guy. The—

"Okay," I said. "What's your fuckin' name, man? I get 'employer' and 'your Honor', but shit on a shingle, dude, throw me a bone here."

He stared at me for a long time. So long, I thought maybe some invisible alien zapped him with a freeze ray or something.

Finally, he snorted. The snort became a laugh. He gestured for me to follow him while he laughed.

"You're a fuckin' weirdo," I said behind him.

The room wasn't massive and actually had that warm feel to it. Like, grandfatherly warm. He sat in a highbacked chair and I plopped down in the pillowy couch across from him.

"My name," he said, smiling. "Ah, yes. There are those who still wish to know names, rather than titles."

"Uh, yeah. Especially since a book is being written right now. I mean, the Author is just rambling on trying to figure out a suitable name for you, douchenozzle. He's getting pissed too. If he kills us all, I blame you and your no-name horseshit."

His smile didn't falter. "It's best you just call me the Employer like everyone else, for now."

I lifted an eyebrow. "The Employer? Seriously? I might as well call you the Butt Plug. C'mon, man, give me something better. The Author just sent me a memo. Wanna know what it says? It says: What the *shit*, people? Because, c'mon!"

He chuckled. "Admiral Burlow said you had a mouth on you."

I paused, not really sure what to say. Finally, I said, "From what I remember, he had the mouth. Anyhoo, name? Don't make me go all pretty-please with a cherry on top cliché shit. Because, I'll fuckin' do it."

"Okay," he said. "If it matters so much, call me Jeff."

I blinked. "Jeff?"

He nodded. "Jeff."

I stared at him. He smiled back.

Gah! "You're lying, but fine. Jeff. Now, what the shit do you want from me, Jeff?"

He shrugged. "To talk."

"To talk—why the fuck are you being so vague?"

"I'm not."

"You are, dickhead."

"Let me explain."

I blew out a breath, puffing out my cheeks. "I've only been waiting since I stepped through the goddamn door, dude."

Jeff chuckled. That guy, he was full of smiles and chuckles, but no real answers. If he didn't give me something soon, I might just bash his—

"We have a situation on Station Uris. As you might know, it is one of the largest stations in the Caliber Galaxy."

"Spit it out, dude."

His smile faded. "The station is infested with Trill bugs. I was contacted by Admiral Burlow to go in and eliminate the bugs, but my specialized teams aren't experienced enough with bugs. The uprisings and tactical work, yes, but an extermination? No."

I grunted. "Your teams sound like idiots."

Jeff frowned. "They are highly sought out by even the Military. They succeed while many do not."

"Yeah? Then why can't they take care of a simple bug problem on an enclosed station. Nowhere for those fuckers to run."

He sighed, uncrossed his legs and sagged forward. "Because they weren't trained to eliminate an infestation." He leveled his gaze on me. "But you are, according to Admiral Burlow."

I stood. "If you're asking me to train your delinquents, get bent. I have better things to do."

"Like living as a crocodile poacher in Australia?"

"Damn fuckin' right. At least I could live without this stigma."

Jeff's eyebrows rose. "Stigma?"

"Oh, stop it. You know what I mean. I'm the greatest intergalactic badass ever. Killed more bugs and intelligent aliens than anybody. That shit carries weight, dude. I might as well be Atlas. Okay, not really, but you get the picture."

With a chuckle, Jeff said, "If it makes you feel any better, I didn't know who you were until Admiral Burlow said something."

I blinked. "So, you don't know what I've done?"

Jeff smiled. "Only a little, from what the Admiral told me. However, it was enough to convince me."

I deflated a bit. It was like being stuck in Australia all over again. How the shit didn't he know who I was? My name was practically splattered all over space, for fuck sake. Seriously, I personally made sure, CLUSTERFUK! THE GREATEST INTERGALACIC BADASS was graphited on every damn waystation and prominent city in every galaxy I found myself stranded in for each and every mission.

How the hell else was one supposed to run a business?

But I digress…

"Fine," I said. "Tell me your terms. I assume you're a tactical militant organization?"

Jeff clapped his hands. "How'd you know?"

I raised an eyebrow. "For shit sake, I hope you're really not that stupid."

He laughed and said, "No. We're not a militant organization. We're a legal merc operation with real soldiers, not wannabes. Every soldier under my employ is highly skilled in their chosen areas. I have over a dozen teams, and each team pulls through despite the odds. The colony of Station Uris, though…it's something they've never encountered."

I stood from the couch. "Where's the team I'll be taking care of?"

***

Jeff, that fantastic bastard, led me to a balcony overlooking a large bay. The bay took up the majority of the lower half of the otherwise relatively small station. Divided, it boasted several areas. A large kitchen, a few tables to eat at, a gym or training area, a gun range, and…

"Dude, is that a fuckin' taco truck?"

Jeff shook his head, crossed his arms. "Apparently."

Hot saliva flooded my mouth. I gazed at the marvelous creature as it made its rounds through the bay. "Sexy."

"Help yourself," Jeff said. "I'll introduce you to the team, give a briefing, and—"

I leaped over the rails and dropped onto the taco truck just as it was passing under. Ca-thump. I left one hell of a dent in the roof too.

Meh. Also, I garnered the attention of pretty much everyone in the bay. Double meh. Because, BURRITOS.

The truck jerked to a stop and I hopped off.

The woman inside, not the driver but the cook, I assumed, gaped at me when I tapped the side of the truck and said, "Triple cheese, beef burrito."

She continued with her infernal gaping.

I sighed. "Okay, sorry I dented your truck but—"

Something struck me hard, like a damn water buffalo, sending me flying. Huh. Did they bring a water buffalo with us too? Weird…

I crashed into a small group of people. They all kind of blinked at me while I laid there trying to figure out where I was. The hit came that hard.

I stood, shaking off the pain of a broken collarbone as it healed. "What the shit was that?"

"Dumplin," a scrawny man said beside me.

I spun on him. "Look, normally I'd be flattered, maybe even take you out on a date, whatever." I straightened. "But I'm not that kind of lady."

"Who the fuck are you?" A voice thundered.

I looked up to find a goddamn behemoth lumbering toward me and the group. I lifted my arms in surrender.

"That's Dumplin," the scrawny dude whispered.

"Hey, thanks for the heads up," I said. "Now get your hand off my ass, perv."

The group slowly backed away as Dumplin stomped his way toward me.

I lowered my arms. Yeah, he wasn't gonna stop. His square face told me that much.

Time for a different tactic. I smiled. "Well, hi there, big fella! Who wants a *hug*?"

"I'm going to rip your arms off and beat you with them, punk."

"You seem nice," I said.

Another six feet and I'd be giant jelly. Giant, indeed. Definitely from the Behemoth Sector on Earth Two. His kind never really forgave humans for settling there and taking most of their land.

Why did that sound so familiar…?

The floor legit shook under my boots, drawing me out of my thoughts just in time to duck a fist the size of an anvil. I back peddled, avoiding another enormous fist. I could heal myself, but it was slow going. He'd kill me before I finished healing.

So, there was only one way to stop him.

I darted around him.

You see, Behemoths were slow bastards. Not turtle slow, but close. If he moved faster, one of those fists would've caught me.

He turned, though by the time he managed to get fully around, I was behind him again.

And…we were drawing quite the crowd. They formed a nice circle around us, like we were gladiators, or something. All it did was encourage the big bastard. He swung around, faster than I anticipated, and nearly took my head off.

Fuck it.

I dashed to the left, sprang onto his back like a spider monkey and slammed both my fists into his ears. A thing I did to the big ones. More or less, it gave them a mild concussion.

He yelped, hands going to his head. I jumped off and backed away. The giant stumbled, dropped to his knees, then collapsed on the floor.

The entire bay fell silent. They still circled me.

I opened my mouth to tell them to all get bent when slow clapping echoed throughout the bay. The people turned their heads, trying to find the source of the clapping.

They didn't need to wait long.

Jeff emerged through a narrow opening between people. He clapped, smiled, and walked toward me.

"Ladies and gentlemen," he said, still clapping. "Clint Clusterfuk."

And the crowd went weird. They all exchanged glances. Mumbles rolled through them. Whispers. I couldn't make anything out, but I assumed they'd heard of me. Well, there you have it. I was fuckin' famous.

What a joke.

Jeff stood in front of me, still clapping. I placed a hand over his clapping ones and said, "I'm not a hero."

He winked. "I know." To the crowd, he said, "Hacksaw Squad, meet me in the briefing room. The rest of you need to be finding some work or get off my station."

The crowd instantly dispersed.

Dumplin, that big goober, he was just snoring away while a few people tried waking him up. Sleeping with a concussion was bad, but…ya know. Whatever.

I followed Jeff to a room just outside the bay and immediately regretted it. An entire platoon stood waiting for us.

I placed a hand on Jeff's shoulder. "I go alone, or no deal."

He snorted. "There hasn't been a deal made yet."

I turned him back outside the room and closed the door. "Maybe some other time with the team thing. This one, I'll go alone."

Jeff frowned. "Why are you telling me this just now?"

"Because, I didn't know what the hell you had planned exactly. I heard team mentioned, but that in there is a goddamn platoon. Too large for what we're gonna be doing. So, here's the deal. Send me in alone with my required gear, and when it's all said and done, I want a lifetime supply of burritos from that gorgeous taco truck over there."

He shook his head. "You want...burritos? I don't think I'm following you. I'm willing to pay you a small fortune to—"

I loomed over him. "It's burritos or nothin', man."

Jeff sighed. "Fine. If you return, will you at least help train the platoon, as you call them?"

"*If* I return? Guuurl, it's *when* I return."

He shook his head again and appeared a bit disgusted. Good. "What is the gear you request?"

"For a bug hunt? A full Supreme Elite suit, minus all the symbols and shit. A C-44 plasma assault rifle with a crate of refill canisters. A tactical impulse shotgun. A magma pistol with extra canisters. A case of sub-nuke grenades. And a partridge in a pear tree."

With a nod, Jeff said, "Those items will require some time to acquire."

"Ask Admiral Droopy Britches to send all that. You'll have it in a couple of hours."

"Admiral who?"

I face-palmed. "Burlow, jackass. Bur-Low."

The man's frown deepened. "You know, I expected more from you."

"Like what? A blowjob? I mean, I haven't swung that way in a few years, but..."

"No. I was told you're an honorable man."

I burst out laughing and couldn't stop. Eventually, Jeff rolled his eyes (like they all do eventually) and walked away.

I shrugged, opened the door to the meeting room. "Never mind. False alarm. Go back to eating tacos and lifting weights."

Speaking of tacos...

NINE

"I'll need to sanitize everything now," the taco truck girl said, slipping back into her uniform.

"Nah," I said and stretched out on the serving counter naked. "I'm clean, babe."

"Don't call me babe."

"Sorry, hotness."

She giggled. "If you weren't so good, I'd kick you out of here."

I grinned.

Her gaze drifted to the clock above me. "Shit. I open in two minutes." She made shooing gestures at me. "C'mon. I need to get ready for the dinner rush."

I gave her a theatrical sigh and hopped off the counter. "Fine. But you owe me a free burrito."

"*Free*?" She glowered at me while she tied her apron on.

Standing in front of her naked, I cocked an eyebrow and planted my hands on my hips. "Who gave you six orgasms in five minutes?"

She opened her mouth and snapped it shut. Finally, she pointed to the rear door. "Fine. Just get out."

"Score," I said, got dressed and departed the taco truck.

When she opened the serving door, I was first in line.

She laughed, shook her head. "What kind?"

"Triple cheese, beef, sexy taco lady."

She favored me with a wink and went to work. I'd have to say she's almost on par with Willie from the Land Down Under. Not as vigorous, but she owned a goddamn taco truck. A taco truck that made burritos too. Willie had a booze-house, this woman (didn't know her name) had the burritos. Win-win in my eyes.

A couple minutes, and she handed me my burrito. Hell, she even deep fried it. I fell in love with her that instant.

"If you're not gone," she said, "I close at eight. Maybe we could hang out at my place?"

I smiled, feeling all sorts of goofy. Was that how love felt? Goofy? I dunno. Never happened to me before. And why the shit was I even thinking about it? I hurried away, sat at a table and unwrapped my pound of cheesy love. She made it perfect. And, with the addition of deep frying it, I almost had another orgasm. The mingling aromas of cheese, beef and oil collided. An explosion I could almost taste. Such savory succulence.

It was still hot from the oil, but my calloused hands barely registered it. I brought the burrito to my mouth.

"Mr. Clusterfuk."

I jumped, nearly dropping the burrito.

Standing directly to my left was Mr. Scott. Lil' Scotty, for short. Kind of. Shut up.

He stood ramrod straight. "My employer sent me to inform you that the items you have requested are in your room."

"Holy fucknuts. Already?"

"Yes."

"Okay. Well, let me finish my burrito and—"

"My employer will be deploying you to Station Uris in approximately twenty minutes. Enough time to gear up and get into a star-pod."

"Fine," I said, standing. "I'll eat on the way to my room."

"Sorry," Lil' Scotty said. "No food allowed in the halls or corridors."

I gave him a withering look. "I'm eating this burrito."

He shook his head. "No. You are not. Eating beyond the bay's perimeter, unless in one's quarters, is strictly forbidden. Punishable by death."

"You...*really*? By *death*? It's a fuckin' burrito, dude. What's it gonna do? Grow wings and ravage the station? Come on..."

"It's my employer's rules."

I went to take a bite.

"You only have fifteen minutes now," Lil' Scotty spouted.

I dropped the burrito in the basket and shoved the son of a bitch out of my way. "Go fuck a rabid donkey, asshat."

He didn't lead me back to my room, nor did I care. I found my way, eventually. How much time did I have? Fuck it.

I should've taken my burrito with me too. Damn it!

When I burst into the room, I found everything I asked for. The Supreme Elite suit stood in an upright nanoglass case.

I ran my fingers over the cool glass and grinned. "Lock'n'load, motherfucker."

***

They all scuttled away from me as I made my way toward the star-pod in a secured section of the station. I wasn't authorized, apparently, but that didn't matter. I used the Station's employee badges as I went.

In my Elite suit, no one dared fuck with me. Full, black body armor. A sealed unit with intakes that produced oxygen constantly, no matter the environment. An exoskeleton, which gave me enhanced strength.

I missed that. Not the oxygen or strength part, though that was cool. I missed everyone scurrying away when I walked into a room.

Looking human was overrated anyway.

People forgot how much of a badass I was.

I ripped a badge from a woman's shirt and slapped it against a scanner. The final door to the star-pods slid open.

"Thanks, beautiful," I said and tossed the badge back to her.

She caught it and actually smiled a little. "Clusterfuk'em up," she said.

I paused. When did that become a thing? Didn't matter, I loved it.

"Wait here, hotness," I said. "I'll be back for you."

She smiled so big I thought she might crack the nanoglass of my helm's visor. I didn't smile. She couldn't see it anyway.

With my crates of ammo, I entered the star-pod, and strapped in.

"Destination Station Uris, commencing," a monotone voice said in the pod. Definitely AI. "Pod launch in: Ten, nine, eight, seven, six, five, four…"

I drew in a breath and blew it out slowly.

"…three, two…"

"Let's do this," I said.

"One."

"Zero."

There came a sudden jolt, though after that, nothing but smoothness, baby. Pods were sexy like that. Smooth and creamy. Mmmm.

With the destination preset for Station Uris, I leaned back in the seat and made myself comfortable.

According to the monitor, I had a good hour before all hell broke loose.

I passed out before I even knew I was tired.

<u>TEN</u>

Thud.

Through the receding foggy veil of sleep, something beeped. But that wasn't what woke me. I've slept through fire alarms louder than that. No, it was more like—

Thud.

—THAT.

Thud.

What the living space shit was *that*?

Thud.

I straightened in the seat and if not for the harness, I would've fallen out and bashed my noggin on the...

"Why am I upside down?" I asked myself, because apparently, I talked to myself now.

Well, not exactly upside down, but close enough. The beeping came from the small control panel of the pod. A red light flashed to the lower left corner. Everything else appeared in working—

Thud.

The pod vibrated that time. I could only see through the front. So, whatever was happening, it must have been either in the back or sides.

Thud.

The pod not only vibrated but rocked.

That's when it dawned on me. The beeping was indeed an alarm, so was the blinking red light. That gave light to what could be happening.

Something was hitting the pod.

Thud.

I eyed the monitor and blew out a long breath too heavy to be a sigh while I read the red flashing words on the otherwise white screen.

LANDING COMPLETE. STATION URIS.

Below the message was another: HOSTILE ENVIROMENT.

I snorted. "No shit? Hostile?"

Thud.

"What was your first clue, bum-nuts?" Damn, I missed Australia.

Thud-clunk.

"Well," I said, "that didn't sound good."

I busted out of the harness and tumbled to the ceiling. I engaged the Elite suit. The helmet's visor booted. Numbers flashed across my vision before clearing. If the suit sensed danger from any direction, the visor would tell me where on the upper right. It also had an aim feature, which connected with the exoskeleton and made aiming dead-on accurate.

A good feature if I felt like sniping, which I couldn't give two wild fucks about. I was more of a burst in and kill'em all kind of dude. Still, sniping a few snipers was always good fun too.

The intakes whooshed. They'd been working the entire time, of course, but in an oxygenated environment. Judging by the dark material I landed somewhere outside the station. The suit was prepping for environmental changes.

I stuffed a pack with ammo. Plasma and canisters, mostly. I fixed the sub-nuke grenades to the magnetic belt of the suit. Likewise, the magma pistol (which is pretty much just a laser, but who's taking notes, right?) I made sure both plasma rifles were fully loaded and engaged and turned to the hatch.

With a rifle in either hand, I smiled. "Time to Clusterfuk'em up."

I slammed a rifle into the release hatch button. It hissed open and, if not for the suit, I would've been yanked right into the claws of a monster. The Elite suit was truly a work of the finest design and craftmanship, though, and planted me into the pod.

The creature shrieked, reached in with a claw that appeared to be made of knives.

"Fuck off." I blasted the bastard directly in its ugly-ass face with both rifles, shredding the claw to bloody ribbons in the process.

In space, nothing fell to the ground. It all floated in the air. Without gravity, shit got really weird bustin' alien skulls. Like intestines and brains and blood, it all just kinda hung out everywhere.

And, of course, that's what happened with the bug I killed. Bits of brain, skull, teeth, gobbets of blood, and burned, tattered gray flesh, it all floated there in front of me.

There was no going around. It'd float there forever in the hatchway of the pod.

"Fuck it," I said and ran through the mess.

It splattered over the visor, obscuring my vison until it all finally lifted away. Guess I could consider that a win for gravity prone cunts like me. Antigravity giveth and taketh away.

Wait, did I just go full Aussie? Cunts? GAH!

Funny how a country, or region of a country, could alter your way of words, and shit. Like, after a year, you're pretty much them now. Throw in the towel. It's fucking over. You're not you. You're them. Craziness. All of it.

It happened to the best of us.

Eventually, the gore lifted off me and rose to grotesque gobbets in the air. Or, rather, non-air. Whatever. It floated, that's all I knew.

The suit did its job, holding me to the station while I made my way to the dock hatch. The outside boasted nothing as far as a way in. No button, or lever. I stood there a second or two, trying to figure out how to get into Station Uris, listening to myself breathe.

I stepped onto a narrow maintenance catwalk, feeling like a moron. I should've studied the station's layout like a good boy. But no. Of course not. Gotta be a badass, right? Badasses don't need to know shitty layouts. We don't need…

A recessed door stood to my left. Of course it did. All the right side boasted was endless space. And an emergency door. Just in case the maintenance folks got stuck outside the station for one reason or another.

The keypad was hidden under a metal flap.

In space, there is sound, but it's too faint for humans to hear. Too minuet. My helm, however picked up the sounds and amplified them at a safe volume for me to hear. And what I heard while I tried to figure out the keycode, was clanking metal. Squeaking metal. The low hum and whoosh of space itself, and the constant hissing.

"Goddamn it."

The proximities sensors beeped. Not just left or right, top or bottom, but everywhere. Every-fuckin-where.

"Ya gotta be fuckin' kiddin' me."

I stepped away from the door and glanced around. I looked a second time, a little slow. Nothing. Just the stupid-ass station in all its black metal glory. (Slow black metal music playing). Okay, that was dumb.

The hissing grew louder. Either it was a combination of space sounds and the station itself, bugs, or I was losing my goddamn mind. Probably all the above.

The sensors beeping quickened until they might as well have been a single, solid bray.

Then, suddenly, it all stopped.

The beeping. The hisses. All of it.

I shook my head and returned to the door.

The beeps kicked up again. The hissing burst into my ears.

"What the actual fuck?" I said and spun around. I looked up and down, in every direction I could and…

"Oh, for fuck sake," I said. "I'm really an idiot."

All the hissing and the sensors were going off because I failed to realize where I stood. The door was recessed a good five feet, which put me directly below the station's upper level, beside the level I stood, and what crawled in the bowels of Uris. Not to mention the sections of the station on the left and right of me.

I heard, and sensed, what lurked beyond the door.

Every keycode I tried, failed.

The door was my only way in. I needed to figure out the code while simultaneously cursing the maintenance dude who set the code in the first place. I mean, whatever the shit happened to 1,2,3,4? Cockgobbler couldn't at least make it a little easy?

That motherfu—

I punched the keypad. Blue sparks exploded into me.

I backed away. "Stupid. Stupid!" I slapped myself. "Bad Clusterfuk. *Bad*!" I glared at the broken keypad sputtering sparks, grinned. "Worth it."

Well, it appeared I needed to figure out a different way in to—

The door stuttered open to utter darkness. Before I could move, it slipped shut again.

Bastard.

It creaked open. Slammed shut.

Three seconds between each movement.

It opened. One. Two. Three.

It slammed shut.

If I got caught between it and the jamb, I'd be stuck. Suit might even take some serious damage, as hard as that door slammed.

"Fuck it." I darted through before the door shut, submerging me in darkness. The suit's tactical light blinked on, giving me a view of the room. Behind me, the door opened and closed. Opened and closed.

The hissing stopped. The beeping stopped. The room boasted six corridor openings. Something which unnerved me a bit.

I needed to get in a better position. Those greasy fucknuts no doubt heard the chattering of the door and they'd be coming to investigate.

Bugs…

Well, as far I knew they were—

They all came at once, flooding the corridors and spilling into the room.

It's Clusterfuk time.

I blasted dozens of the bugs into green goop before they came within twenty feet of me. They moved like nothing I ever encountered, though. Like black liquid, they flowed through the corridors. They crawled across the ceiling, along the walls, and swarmed over the floor. They moved like a singular mass.

That was how bugs defeated armies. They swarmed. They worked together, collectively. They didn't stop until their enemy was consumed. Literally. Bugs, no matter what the species, loved to eat. Not a pretty sight after a bug swarm passed through. In fact, I was pretty sure it was a bug that attacked my family that night long ago. The one whose blood will forever be a part of me. The only monster I could never get rid of, no matter how hard I tried.

I couldn't tell you how many times I'd been shot to shit before, pretty much a mound of bloody pulp, and, within a couple of days rise to fight another day. So weird being mush and suddenly feeling yourself fuse back together and reconstruct. It stung, by the way, when your body reconstructed itself. If you didn't know it, you might even go mad during it all.

Luckily for me, I didn't go crazy.

Or did I?

Crazy people didn't know they were crazy, right?

Wait…

Shit.

The bugs in Uris were different, though. They acted collectively, and yet attacked individually. Not one lashed out the same. Well, as far as I could tell. I was kinda fuckin' busy.

I slapped a plasma rifle onto the magnetic plate on my back and clenched my right hand. The retractable blade shot out. A long, serrated thing with a nice, wicked point and an edge so sharp it'd cut through bone.

They had me surrounded on all sides. Hissing and growling. Their gray skin gleamed in the lights given off by the suit. They didn't have eyes set in their oblong heads, from what I could tell. There was something almost feline in the way they moved. Graceful…deadly. Calculating. The skin of their mouths peeled away from white, needle-like teeth with every hiss or growl. Arms, longer than their legs, boasted black claws probably just as sharp as my retractable blade.

And…did I mention I was completely surrounded? Top, all sides. Only the floor for about ten feet away was clear. There was no escape. No room for fuck-ups either.

"Alright," I said, projecting my voice through the helm's mic to the outside. "Let's get one thing straight." I tucked the plasma rifle in my left hand between my right arm and body. "I don't do gangbangs, okay? All you guys comin' up on me all slobbery." I pointed at one closest to me. "Especially you, drool cakes. I mean, c'mon. Least ya could do is ask first." I pulled a sub-nuke (atomic, whatever) grenade from the magnetic belt and pulled the pin. "It's just bad. Comes over all rapey, ya know?"

They didn't even appear to notice the grenade in my hand.

I stepped toward the larger mass on the left. "Cool? We all good? Yeah?" I tossed the grenade into the mass of gray creatures. "Because I don't condone rape, you miserable cunts."

I pulled the plasma rifle out from between my arm and body, crouched low and let the fuckers on the ceiling have it.

The hisses switched to shrieks. Yellow blood rained down on me. Still low, I spun and took out as many bugs to the right and in front of me as possible. Then—

Boom.

The grenade went off. The blast sent me pummeling into the mass on the right. I took out more than a few without even trying and crashed into a wall. No damage to the suit, as far as the sensors told me.

I stood and blinked. What wasn't dead twitched and howled in agony on the floor. Most were missing limbs. Others crawled around whining; the lower half of their body gone. Green guts trailed out behind them. Everything was splashed with yellow gore. Including myself.

I wiped the helm's visor as best I could and went about killing the injured.

I keep forgetting how powerful those damn grenades were.

Guess they really meant it when they said, "atomic" and "sub-nuke". Why the shit doesn't that ever register with me?

Eh, oh well.

I sloshed through the yellow, gray and green mess and entered one of the six corridors. There was only one mission. And that mission was: Kill'em all.

I missed Australia, but I think I missed kill'em all missions more.

The corridor gradually sloped downward before leveling off a bit. Steam seeped from a few broken pipes on the ceiling, creating a surreal, creepy environment. There were no lights on. Just my suit's lamps. Beyond their reach, everything was darkness. I felt like I was in some sci-fi horror movie. With the swirling steam and darkness…yeah, kinda scary.

But, fuck it. Do or die now.

I picked up the pace, jogging down the corridor, not caring how much noise I made.

Eventually, I entered a large room that could only be described as a mess hall, or cafeteria. Tables and chairs took up most of the place, from what I could tell. Beyond that was a long counter with glass sneeze shields. Like an old Subway when I was a kid. Anyway, the counter was where people got their food. And, as I moved closer, I spotted the kitchen behind the counter.

A weird cry echoed through the cafeteria.

I caught a glimpse of something jump off a table and scuttle toward the long counter. Plasma rifle raised, I ventured deeper into the cafeteria. Whatever was in there with me, it wasn't very big. And, as far as I knew, the only one. I still had a job to do, though. Which meant blasting that little bastard to gooey pulp.

The cafeteria was spacious enough to create echoes, so I stopped and listened. I scanned the area where I last spotted the creature. No sounds. No movement. Whatever it was, it knew how to conceal itself.

Well…it had never met a Clusterfuk before…

I opened fire along the counter. The light blue bursts of the plasma illuminating the entire area for a few seconds and—

There.

It scrambled away from the counter and cowered under a table. I blasted the table to smithereens. The creature darted away in a classic zig-zag formation all the way to the other side of the room. A good one hundred feet. And, of course, it was too far for my lights to reach.

I stormed forward, flipping tables out of the way as I went. The little fucker was really pissing me off.

With nowhere else to run, I found it quivering in a corner. It wasn't one of the bugs I killed upon entering the station. Christ, it resembled a puppy more than anything. Granted, a furless, blue puppy, but still. Its large eyes gaped at me with utter horror.

My finger began to squeeze the trigger of the plasma rifle.

It mewled, body shivering in utter fear.

If I had been a year younger, I would've blown the little bastard to bits. But, right then, all I could do was point the rifle at it and do nothing. No matter how much I tried to make my finger behave and blast it all to hell, my finger refused to obey.

Note to self: Cut finger off for treason.

I lowered the gun with a heavy sigh. It perked up a bit. Its big eyes blinked at me.

"Goddamn it," I said. "Just stay out of the way, okay?"

It blinked.

Of course, it didn't know what the hell I was saying, but I hoped my tone eased it a bit.

Maybe not all alien bugs were a threat on the Uris. Which made me wonder, what the living shit happened? Some lab experiment gone wrong? They tricked dock supervisors into accepting an alien seed vessel? Seed vessels were an inventive, though common attack from alien entities. Send a shuttle loaded with spores and parasites and eggs. Eventually, someone will open it. And then…

I turned away from the small creature and broke through a door, exiting the cafeteria.

ELEVEN

In another corridor, albeit much larger than the last, I ejected the nearly spent canister of my plasma rifle and slapped a fresh one in. With a straightening of the wrist, the blade slipped back into the suit's right forearm.

The corridor turned this way and that until I came to a room, though not quite as large as the cafeteria. Massive screens took up four walls. Took me a bit to get it. The room was like a theater, or common room for its residents. For employees though, not the general population. Much too small for that.

A closer look at the room revealed something more.

Bodies. Or rather, scattered remains. Limbs and heads, partially eaten torsos. Blood was splashed on each screen. Intestines were strewn over the seats like gruesome Christmas garlands.

I sighed and made my way to one of two, besides the one to the corridor I came from. Locked. Need a passkey.

"Lovely."

I stormed across the room, stomping through guts and crushing skulls under my heavy boots.

Both doors were likewise locked.

"Wankers." I blinked. "Did I really just say, 'wankers'? Goddamn it, yes I did."

I turned to the mess splattered throughout the room.

They were all employees. Which meant…

A breath too heavy to be a sigh blew out me. "Here we go, boys and girls. Scavenger hunt."

I dug through the guts and blood-soaked clothing. Through the spilled brains and severed limbs.

"Oh, for fuck sake," I said. "Was it leave your pass at home day, or something?"

I was about to just kick in a door when I turned and spotted the upper half of a man slumped against the wall. His lower jaw was missing, leaving strings of red and a mauled tongue. I also got a good view into his throat.

Below all that though, hanging on a lanyard, was a passkey. I yanked on the passkey, but it didn't come free as I hoped. Instead, the dude's mutilated face smacked into my groin. I didn't feel it, because, Elite suit, but…I mean, COME ON.

I ripped the damn passkey over the dead dude's head and kneed him away. He thumped against the wall, slid slowly onto his side.

I slapped the bloodstained passkey onto the scan pad. The door didn't open.

Then, I remembered, the power was out. Good gods of chunky peanut butter, I was an idiot.

"I blame Australia."

I stepped back and slammed a boot into the door. It buckled a bit but held.

I kicked the metal door twice more before it gave out, tore off its hinges, and crashed into the wall opposite me. Now, there was something. Door hinges weren't a thing in space. Everything slid up and down and side to side. Doors set deep in the floor and ceiling on tracks. Way of the future, or some shit. Well, not so much future anymore. Figured they would've come up with something more fitting for the new age, but, nope. Of course not. Lazy bastards.

The hallway I stepped into, though darker than the corridors, greeted me with more blood and guts.

My lips pressed together.

The aliens on the station were fierce assholes, that was for sure.

Plasma rifle ready, I walked down the hall. Only the sound of my own heavy footfalls kept me company.

It was too narrow to be a corridor, so, I guess it would be a hallway?

Right?

Sure.

Boom.

There were no doors, just a long, dark tube leading to more darkness.

I picked up the pace, because, well, the walking shit was getting boring.

The door at the end of the hall was open. I moved over the threshold into a room full of dead monitors and empty desks. Communications, of some sort, would be my guess. Each station had like ten communication departments. Running a station, especially the size of Uris, took a lot of communication, organization, and teamwork.

All that happy crappy.

Ah, but bonus. Only a couple of eviscerated bodies in that room. There were two levels of the room. The upper, where I stood, and a lower, which was down a short flight of stairs. As far as I could tell, there weren't any bugs down there.

Speaking of bugs, where the hell were they? Or, did I kill all the ugly bastards in the beginning? If so…son of a bitch. I wanted more than that. Expected more than that. Needed more than that.

I kicked open a door, stepped through and came face to stomach with a monster.

It towered over me, that thing. Its flabby, greasy yellow belly rippled and made a weird groan.

I darted backward, looking up just in time to avoid what appeared to be a scorpion pincer from snapping my head off. The groaning of the belly turned to growling. I backed into the comms room to gather my bearings.

Thick gurgling filtered through the open doorway. A pincer shot through, snapped, darted back into darkness.

"What the shit are you?" I asked.

Of all the creatures I'd encountered, that fat bastard took the cake. I couldn't pin it on a species I knew. Where the hell did it come from? It all made me feel like the station was targeted. Release bugs into a station with unarmed people…no more station.

The monster roared. It slammed itself into the wall with the doorway, making dents in the metal.

Its flabby belly jiggled in front of the doorway.

I grinned. "Santa Claus is comin' to town, motherfucker."

I sprinted forward, triggered the retractable blade and swiped it through the creature's belly. Blue blood trickled then, as the cut split open into a gaping gouge, blue tinged guts spilled out onto the floor.

The creature screamed. It staggered away from the doorway, guts unraveling as it backed up.

"Bitchin'," I said and ran through the doorway to finish it off.

Before I could fire a shot though, one of its pincers snapped around me, pinning my gun arm to my body. It screamed. It was dying, and yet…it wouldn't die without taking me with it.

It lifted me so that we were face to face.

Its fat, snapping maw filled with jagged, yellow teeth. Its three, amber eyes. It was uglier than a goddamn Solite. Its yellow skin glistened and, I imagined, if I touched it, my hand would come away covered in putrid slime.

PRESSURE WARNING, blinked on the left side of my visor.

I glared at the creature. "You, sir, are an asshole."

I plunged the arm blade into the center eye. Amber goo burst from the eye socket, followed by blue blood. It sprayed all over me. Because, of course it did.

The pincer spasmed, opened, and I dropped to the floor.

I didn't give the putrid bastard another chance and blew its ugly head off with my plasma rifle. Boom. Splatter. Dead.

It fell backward, body twitching for a second or two before falling still.

"Christ, dude," I said trying to wipe its blood from the visor so I could see. "Whatever you are, you bleed like a stuck hog."

With my suit being of eternium alloy, wiping the blood away was easier said than done. I needed a goddamn rag, or something. I ventured back into the comms room, tore off the cleanest shit I could find, and managed to clean the visor enough to see clearly.

The suit had a burn away feature, which literally burned away the blood or dirt, or whatever got on the visor. But it took a minute and drained the power. I'd be a sitting duck until the power rejuvenated. If I could find a secure room, maybe I'd do it the right way.

For now, though…

I tossed the shirt aside and walked through the doorway. I rounded the big dead bastard and continued on my way.

Back to a corridor again. Much higher, wider, and…

"Fuck."

They scuttled toward me on crablike legs, moving as agile as spiders. Clackclackclackclack. Their shelled legs on the metal floor was unnerving, even for me.

They reached out with char-black, humanlike arms and hands. Between those arms was a snapping beak which reminded me of a snapping turtle. It shot out, that beak, like a striking snake.

Six of them in all.

Plasma rifle blasting its pale blue rounds, I roared. The first two lost a couple of legs and clattered to the floor, mewling. They scrambled, trying to stand, while the other four crawled over them. I blasted those fuckers too, though not fast enough. Their momentum sent them hurtling at me.

I sprinted at them, dropped and slid underneath the first one. With a quick jab, I stabbed the retractable blade into its stomach. Or chest. Whatever.

I soon recognized the bastards. Ticks. Originally from the outward planet, Zeldum. No relation to wood ticks from Earth, of course. One of my missions with the Skull Daggers took place there. If ever there was a definition of a bug, they were it.

I slit the tick right down the middle, spilling, not guts exactly, but certainly its vital shit. All, more or less, translucent.

Still sliding, I found myself under another and cut a deep gash in it too.

I skidded to a stop on my back and stood. With a quick glance, the two I cut open were already down. Not moving. Dying or dead.

The remaining two, however, moved independently. A thing not at all common with ticks. Which struck me dumbfounded for a second while one of them scuttled on the wall to get behind me and the other reared up like a pissed off tarantula.

"Doing the tricky tick, eh?"

Trying to distract me.

I fell to a crouch, spun, and blasted the one behind me into crabmeat. I turned to the other just in time to plunge the retractable blade into its soft middle. Translucent innards squirted out like a popped pimple.

It shrieked, bashed itself against the wall, then dropped at my boots. Dead.

I grunted, climbed over them and carried on.

Because, fuck 'em.

TWELVE

I took a wrong turn somewhere because I found myself smack-dab right in the shitty middle of a nest.

Another species I wasn't familiar with.

Whoever, or whatever, sent the spores, eggs, and gods knew whatever else, they were reaching and made sure exotic creatures were involved too. Because it shocked and took people, even the military, off guard. Hell, the Governs (HOB Galaxy Government) didn't send the military to exterminate stations anymore. They hired expendable teams. Like the Skull Daggers, and so many more. They didn't want the blood on their hands, in other words.

The creatures held residence in a room much larger than the cafeteria. Blanketed with egg pods and strange, red webs, I couldn't tell what the room used to be. A gym, maybe?

It was so well constructed I didn't realize where I walked until I noticed the red webbing. From there, I noted the thousands of egg pods.

I stopped walking and looked around for the best way to escape. Only thing I spotted was a door about one hundred feet ahead, though draped in red webs.

I'm no expert, but if a web was disturbed, wouldn't that alert the spiders, or whatever the fuck occupied the maybe gym?

Shit, I felt like a noob soldier. All nervous and jumpy. Not scared though. Shit, even when I was a noob, I didn't scare easily.

I blamed Australia…

Okay, not really. But I did blame my childhood. I mean, who got over a bug slaughtering your family, then killing said bug only to gain some weird healing and strength ability? My family were torn apart before my very eyes, and there I was. Not able to move until the monster came at me. If only I had done something to stop it before. Maybe my parents would still be alive. Maybe I wouldn't be who I was today.

It's what I deserved for being a coward.

Survivor's guilt was a motherfucker.

Carefully, I made my way down the narrow passage toward the door. I was considered crazy, but, shit, I didn't even know what I was dealing with yet. I could only be crazy if I at least had an inkling to what wanted to eat me. And, maybe I was as crazy as people thought. Typically, I didn't care what a bug or alien could do to me. As long as I made sure they were dead. If people saw that as crazy, well, then…I was a batshit nutball.

Soft chitters floated through a small opening in the red weds to the right.

I swallowed a thick lump in my throat and continued to the door.

More chitters rose out of the silky webs surrounding me. Webs which entangled themselves around the egg pods.

The stuff didn't cover the door, but rather hung over it. Like a fucked up veil.

The chitters grew louder, becoming a sound that reminded me of a rattlesnake. I turned back to the room.

Not good.

Subtle movement behind a large, red bundle caught my eye not far in a slight rise off the floor. The entire massive room rose and fell like foothills.

And all of it, for as far as the lights on my suit could reach, moved.

I drew the other plasma rifle from the backplate magnet and said, "Okay, you bastards. Let's do this."

Both guns were fully charged. Ready to go.

I squeezed the triggers.

Bright, pale blue bursts of plasma energy shot out in rapid fire. I turned back and forth, spraying the shots, obliterating everything directly in front of me and to my flanks.

I didn't have time to work on the hills across the building.

They dropped onto me from the ceiling. Dozens of them. Their teeth made constant clanking noises on my suit. I thrashed, kicking and tossing them off.

They squealed at me, all crouched down, lower jaws unhinging. Small, pointy teeth glinted in the suit's lights. They weren't spiders. Not even close. More humanoid in structure. They crawled around like feral things. Their red skin rippled with every movement. Their hands were wide, stubby claws. All humanoid aspects stopped with the head, however. It was more snake-like. Arrowhead shaped, like a viper. Their eyes reflected light as all nocturnal animals did.

The rattling noise didn't come from a tail, though. It spewed out their gaping mouths.

More of them spilled out of the hills across the gym.

I grunted. "Well, now. Looks like you ugly fucknuts need a good Clusterfuking."

They squealed at me with their long mouths and small teeth, and reflective eyes and…fuck it.

I opened fire, blasting all of them in front of me to steaming, red goo.

Speaking of red, how the hell did they—

One of them scampered up to me and spat red webbing into my face, blanketing my goddamn visor.

Ah. That's how…

"You little cumbum," I said, throwing it off me and peeled the webbing from the visor only to find the rest of them surging at me like a tsunami with teeth and claws.

"Really?" I managed before they spilled over me.

My suit beeped. Pressure warnings blasted across the visor. Even a minor damage warning popped up.

They piled on me. Shit, I didn't know how many. All I knew was darkness and the warning beeps of the suit.

I let them pile on.

The more, the merrier.

And, I was gonna regret this…

I slipped a sub-nuke grenade from the magnetic belt and pulled the pin. The suit had taken minor damage, but what would happen if it took a full-on grenade blow? Soldiers died in those suits. Not from the bomb penetrating, but from the severe pressure shutting the life support system down. Clogging of the oxygen intakes. Whatever. People just died from it. Personally, I was never that stupid. Until right then…

How many seconds were left? Five? Three?

I shoved the grenade into the mess above me and waited to die.

With an explosion like that, it wouldn't matter how well I healed. It'd pulverize me into oblivion even inside the suit.

And yet, when it came, I was a bit underwhelmed.

Heat baked through the suit, though nothing more than the hot burst from opening an oven door. Intense at first followed by a radiating warmth. The warmth soon faded and still I found myself in darkness.

WARNING: INTAKE CLOGGED, my visor read.

Ugh.

I stood, ashes falling away from me in gray mounds. It swirled the air, obscuring my vision.

WARNING: INTAKE CLOGGED.

"Yeah, yeah," I said. "Keep your panties on."

I could get away with one clogged intake, but I'd still have to beat my head against a brick wall while my helm and visor continuously reminded me. So…

"Emergency oxygen burst," I commanded the suit.

OXYGEN BURST COMMENCING, the visor read.

As soon as the pressure made my ears pop, I held my breath. A loud whoosh rocked me.

Bursts sucked. During the entire process, you couldn't breathe. You needed to keep your eyes closed too, because your eyeballs might get sucked right out of their sockets. Fuckin' gruesome shit, man. Saw it a couple of times.

A soft flump, and all the pressure dropped inside the suit.

I clamped my eyes and mouth shut. I waited. And goddamn if it didn't take hours before pressure finally equalized and all intakes functioned again. All the pent up air in my lungs blew out of me. I sounded like a balloon with the last of its air escaping through the lip. Like a weak fart, I guess.

"Who the fuck are you?"

I blinked, spun, and gaped at a purple skinned woman. Head to toe…holy HOTNESS. No doubt she came from the planet Tulleev still within the HOB Galaxy. Great place to go on vacation to when you get leave in the military. A hotspot, actually. For its scenery, beauty, serenity…and the hot women. Ah, hell, let's not discriminate. The men were hot too. It was just a big fucking ball of sexiness.

"Well," I said, "Hi there, gorgeous."

She frowned. "Who are you? What do you want?"

"Clint Clusterfuk. Here to exterminate the threat and probably bang you later."

Her face was slightly longer than a human's; mouth, far too wide. Her nose, too narrow, barely a blade of grass. Other than those minor things though, her body was smokin' hot. Nice and curvy, just how I liked'em.

"Excuse me?" She lifted a laser pistol.

"Did I stutter? Shit…maybe I did. I have this weird condition when I get nervous around hot girls that I just—"

She shot me square in the chest.

MINOR DAMAGE: CHEST, the vision informed me.

"Hey," I said. "Calm your moist nuggets, lady. I'm here to help."

She kept the gun pointed at me. Didn't say anything.

"Are there any other survivors? And how the shitweasel are you able to breathe right now?"

Like most humanoids, a Tulleevian needed oxygen in the air.

She cocked a dark eyebrow. "Same reason why everything isn't floating. The gravity and air still function."

Aaaand, I'm an idiot. I should've known that. But…

"Hey, I was a little fuckin' busy killing bugs, okay? Cut me some slack."

She lowered the pistol. "Where's the rest of you?"

I snorted. "Oh, I'm all here, baby."

She cringed. "I mean your team, asshole. Where's your team?"

"Oh! Well, in that case." I made my voice sound all sultry. "I'm all here, baby." She couldn't see my face through the visor, but I grinned anyway.

"You?" She laughed a little. "You're just one guy. And what kind of name is Clusterfuk, anyway?"

I shrugged. "It's Norwegian. Look, sexiness, we can jabber here all day, or go to wherever you've been holed up and relieve some tension…if ya know what I mean."

She holstered her pistol, spun, and walked away.

What wasn't in ashes lay in bloody ruin around me.

"Nice work clearing out the room, though," she said, stepping through the doorway. "We'll be seeing their bigger brothers anytime now with all the noise you've made."

I caught up to her. "Look, I'm not here to fuck around, no matter how much you want me. I'm the fuckin' exterminator, lady."

She spun on me. I almost plowed her over with my momentum. The Elite suit saved me that embarrassment. Full stop.

"Jesus lickin' a lollipop," I spouted. "Warn a dude before you slam on the brakes."

"I don't know who you think you are," she said. "But I'm not a slut like most of my species. I don't want you. What I want is to get off this station and settle on Earth Two. That's *all* I want. Understand?" She turned around and continued walking.

But, gods on fire, that was an amazing ass…

I shook my head. C'mon, Clusterfuk. Get your head in the game and stop drooling over the woman.

Easier said than done, but, ya know…gotta get your priorities straight before something—

It burst out of a vent high up in the wall and pounced on top of the woman before I had a chance to lift a plasma rifle.

It resembled a furless wolf with a ridiculously long tail and taut, pink skin.

The tail lashed like a bullwhip.

The woman screamed.

"Shit." I triggered the retractable arm blade and ran at the creature.

I plunged the blade into its side, lifted it above my head and flung the bastard down the hall. The damn thing landed about ten feet away. I turned my attention to the woman. Silvery blood slathered her neck and chest, but I couldn't find a wound. She whined, head lolling back and forth.

A growl shook me, even through the suit. I lifted my gaze to find another furless wolf-like beast stalking toward me out of the shadows, green eyes glowing. The upper lip of its muzzle peeled back to reveal long, pointy teeth. Its head lowered. The only thing wolf-like about it was the body and head. Even then, it was a bit of a stretch. Everything sleek and smooth, it didn't even have ears.

It moved closer, head down, green eyes fixed on me. Its grizzly bear claws clicked on the metal floor.

I pointed the plasma rifle at it. "I don't have time for theatrics, bruh." I squeezed the trigger. The blast blew the creature to bloody ribbons.

That wasn't a bug. Whatever it was, it appeared to be mutated. An alien species, sure, but…altered, maybe? Shit, I didn't know. And it wasn't my job to know. My job was the simple one.

Seek and fuckin' destroy.

I knelt beside the woman. She stared at the ceiling; eyes glossy.

"Check vitals," I ordered the suit, sent the blade back to its home and placed a hand on her chest.

A long beep sounded. A short beep. A couple of bleeps. And…
SUBJECT: DECEASED.

I sighed, stood and moved on.

We weren't far from a door propped up with a two-foot long metal pipe. Too narrow for me to fit through. I gripped the bottom of the door, kicked the pipe out of the way and lifted the door up. I stepped through and let the door fall.

Clank.

If that drew more bugs, aliens, mutated werewolves…so be it.

I stood in a wide corridor, doors lining either side. Despite its width, it didn't go on for long. The other door, closed, was less than fifty feet away. Living quarters, but surely not for all the employees.

I opened the first door and paused. A younger man hung from a pipe in the ceiling, a steel cable wrapped around his neck. His eyes bulged from their purple sockets. His black tongue hung out a yawning mouth with small teeth. His skin wasn't purple, just his face. The rest was gray.

I knew the alien species too. A Celiubrus. Christ, I thought those bastards went extinct years ago. Constant, massive wars on their planet, Galgo, took out most of them from what I heard. A species bred in war and…died in war.

Apparently, the stories I heard were bullshit.

My gaze lowered his blue uniform. The badge on the right side of the chest. An Intergalactic Marshalls badge.

Badasses, though too law abiding for my taste.

I closed the door and checked the next room. That one was empty. I walked around it for a moment, spotted a similar uniform and the same badge.

It made sense why the living quarters were so small. It housed the Marshalls. They must've been like the law enforcement on Uris. Which also explained why the Tulleev woman carried a laser pistol.

Gah. Too much thinking going on. I made my way to the door on the other side of the corridor.

I kicked it down and stepped into chaos.

THIRTEEN

The area I found myself in was enormous. A vast cavern.

With all the craziness, it took me longer than it should have to realize it was the loading bay. Right below me was a supply trailer, though splashed with blood and human body parts.

I stood on a high platform. Catwalks stretched out from either side of me. And in front of me…a world of madness.

Creatures and bugs scuttled and crawled along the floor. A few blue blobs with teeth floated through the air. Things that resembled gigantic bats soared every which way. Large, lumbering beasts bashed smaller bugs and ate them.

Assuming everyone in the station was dead, they were getting hungry. Ravenous.

The larger monsters were feeding off the smaller already. Soon, it'd be every creature for itself. Species would turn on each other. They'd go cannibal.

I didn't know what the rest of Uris held, but it appeared a majority of the creatures were locked in the bay.

I could have just stepped back into the living quarters, knocked down the other door and figured out a way to check out the rest of the station, but…what fun would that be?

I pulled my spare plasma rifle from the magnetic plate on my back and blew out a breath. I backed into the living quarters, made sure both plasma canisters were full, and sprinted through the doorway.

I leaped over the railing. "Surprise, motherfuckers!"

I swept the plasmas, blindly, back and forth, up and down, even diagonally until I landed on the supply trailer. The force, plus my weight, buckled the top of the supply trailer.

Screams and shrieks and howling erupted through the bay.

Welp. No turning back now.

I hopped off the supply trailer, landing directly on a scurrying crab-like bug. It splattered in green goo.

The floating blue blobs with teeth all jetted toward me. I blasted them until I realized the plasmas were doing little damage to the bastards.

I ran toward the center of the bay, turning every bug and creature that came at me to splatter. Something slammed into me from the right. A fuckin' bug no larger than a dog. It dug its spiny legs into the suit, snapped its three toothy mouths at me.

"Eat cock," I said, slammed the muzzle of my left plasma into its face, and blew the ugly thing to kibbles.

"Antigravity boots, engage."

I jumped and shot into the air. Below me, dozens of alien beasties collided into each other. Blood and guts exploded upward. They thrashed and hacked and chomped at each other.

It was fucking beautiful.

One of those blue blobs with teeth greeted me. Red tentacles shot out of its misshapen body and wrapped around me before I could shoot it. Slowly, I was drawn toward an ever-gaping maw lined with rows of jagged, yellow teeth. A thin, wiggling tongue awaited me eagerly.

"It's time to abort your entire fucking species, douchenugget."

I triggered the arm blade, which sliced through the tentacles holding that arm, and plunged the blade between the creature's beady, black eyes. It screeched. The tentacles slipped back into its blubbery, blue body. I twisted the blade. Its screeching rose to near deafening decibels before it sagged and fell silent. I yanked the blade out and the alien dropped like a stone to the floor. The bastards swarmed over it.

"Dinner is served," I said, lowering.

To keep the anti-gravity boots working, I needed to jump every now and then. Otherwise I'd slowly drop to the floor. So, I jumped, keeping myself in the air and well above the mess below.

One of those bat-like monsters darted at me, lower jaw unhinging like a snake, ready to scoop me up and take me away to feed on, no doubt. I drifted aside, just in time, and swung the arm blade, severing its bulbus, green, shimmery head. Black blood gushed, trailing upward while the body fell. The head soon followed.

Again, those hungry assholes down there were all over the corpse. Fresh meat. I guess, if I was starving, I'd be the same way. You're human? Well, shit…that sucks. Boom. And on the spit over a fire you go.

Heh. Okay, maybe not.

But maybe…

In a second, I found myself in darkness and my visor screaming: PRESSURE WARNING.

What the shit?

I turned and, with help from my suit's lights, stared down a wide esophagus. It took me a second, but…

Holy shit pebbles! Something just ate me!

Never, in all the years of busting alien skulls, had I been eaten. And for good reason.

ALL INTAKES CLOGGED, my visor scrolled.

"Oh, for fuck sake," I said and slashed the arm blade.

I burst out of the thing that ate me in a mess of gore and watched it tumble to the floor. One of the blue blob creatures.

Fuckin' wanker.

Since there wasn't much matter clogging the intakes, the suit blew them out no problem.

I spun just before another blue blob swallowed me up. I sprang and buried the blade into one of the alien's black eyes. It screamed. I yanked the blade out and sliced most of its flabby face off.

It twitched and eventually fell to join its mates on the floor and the smorgasbord going on down there.

I took out the last of the blue blobs before something struck me. Hard. So hard, it sent me flying into the wall. My visor blinked, revealing I only had forty percent shield now. Good thing it was a station and not a ship, otherwise I'd be barreling around in space right then. Thin walls, and such. A station was more structurally sound. Well, more or less. Depended on the manufacturer.

I began falling toward the floor. Below me, the bugs and alien monsters gathered, awaiting their next meal.

A howl drew my attention upward.

One of those bat things shot toward me.

I jumped in midair. I ascended away from the wall in less than two seconds, spun, and shot a couple of plasma bursts at the bat-thing. One of the shots caught its right wing, blowing it into smithereens.

It squawked, left wing flapping. It spiraled to the floor where the others quickly consumed it.

One thing I noted, however, even through battle, the larger monsters didn't move from across the bay. They watched me. That, in itself, unnerved me a bit. Felt like they were planning something. Or memorizing my moves. All in all, it was just fuckin' creepy.

They were like gigantic bodybuilders with large bumpy heads and gaping mouths. Their long tongues lashed out, flicked the air (or snatched up a nearby critter) and slipped back into their mouths. Spikes littered the crowns of their oddly shaped heads and boulder-like shoulders. White skinned and utterly grotesque looking.

Those were the monsters I needed to be aware of. The big white ones with the gaping maws and lashing tongues.

Another bat-thing slammed into me, carrying me upward with a shriek toward the station's ceiling.

"Time for the boom, assboil," I shouted and blasted the fucker with the plasma rifle.

A spray of violet blood rained down. Its body soon followed. Still, the behemoths across the bay remained still. They watched. They learned.

I hated species that did that shit. Made them too close to human. Although, there were trillions of species out there far more intelligent than humans. Which was why they lived peaceful lives outside of the HOB Galaxy. They were even smart enough to realize we'd all just kill each other eventually, like we did on Earth. So...what was the point in taking over when your adversary was the equivalent of the old candy, chocolate? All melty and shit.

Anyway, back to those big fuckers across the bay...

I wondered, what would happen when I finally touched the floor? Would they come at me then...or wait until all the other creatures were killed? Honestly, I hoped they waited till the end. Because, dealing with all the other fuckers, and they come lumbering in...yeah...that'd be crazyflakes, dude.

If there were more bat-things, they either slept or were too scared to come at me. Just as well. But, if they decided to fuck things up while battling the big, white assholes across the way...I might just take the helmet off and bite out their throats.

Okay, that was gross. Sorry kids!

All the flying aliens taken care of, I drifted. Not to the floor, but the catwalk. Opposite the other end of the bay where the big assholes remained, flicking their weird tongues out and acting like thugs controlling their block in some ancient American documentary, or something. They never looked away from me.

The other creatures below were still interested in the small meals I gave them.

I changed the plasma canisters. Four more left. Fan-fucking-tastic. Welp, looked like I needed to get a bit more creative.

Until then, though...

I aimed the plasmas at the biggest bastard. Needed to be dead on. Those things could no doubt reach the catwalks. All it took was one good pull and the walks would be torn down. I didn't know how fast they moved, either. Walking around, they appeared slow, but looks were pretty damn deceiving.

My visor locked on to its head. The suit guided my arms for accuracy. I drew in a breath, blew it out slow and sque—

"No," a voice whispered behind me. "Leave them alone. Let them starve."

I lowered the plasmas and turned, coming face to face with a four-armed alien. Genderless, its oval head boasted two very buggy black eyes and a small slit for a mouth. It was blue. All of it. Well, save for the uniform. The Intergalactic Marshalls badge forced a sigh out of me.

"Can't they get up here?" I asked.

It shook its head. "Too weak. Could not before when they were sealed in."

I spun back to the monster. "Oh, c'mon. Can't I just peck a few off from here?"

"They are of no threat." A pause. "The threat is near the station's core."

I glanced over my shoulder. "A threat, you say?" I whirled around. "Well, then…lead the way Quadranuts!"

Both big eyes blinked. "I do not follow you."

I sighed. "Well, you're gonna be a lot of fun." I gestured toward a door propped open with a pipe, much like the other one.

"You guys ever think about maybe, I dunno, turning the fucking power back on?"

My new Marshall friend stopped at the door. "The threat is near the core. We cannot turn the power on without getting to the core. Only environmental systems remained working."

"Why?"

It blinked at me. "We do not know." Then it slipped under the narrow gap at the foot of the door.

I sighed. "Of course you don't."

I lifted the door open, kicked the pipe aside and let the door drop.

Clank.

Déjà vu?

Oh, yeah, right, I did the same thing when entering the Marshalls' living quarters. Idiot.

"Why isn't Bird with you?" a female of Tulleev origins, judging by her purple complexion and long face, asked.

"Bird?" I knew they couldn't see my expression, but I cocked an eyebrow anyway. I knew who she was, of course. Sometimes I liked to act all oblivious just to mess with people. Never failed.

"Yeah, asshole," the Tulleev woman said. Not as hot as Bird, but…I'd still bang her. "Bird. My sister. Where the fuck is she?"

"Oh," I said. "You got fire. I like that."

She drew her laser pistol and placed the muzzle against my visor. "Look, Captain Idiot. Either you tell me where she's at or I blow a hole through you right now."

I grunted. "Go ahead. The beam won't make it through the shield."

"This is an R-Revol—"

I snatched the pistol out of her hand, tossed it aside, and triggered the arm blade. It shot out with a stealthy, *shink*.

"Okay," I said, "Toughgirl. I'm Clint Clusterfuk and I'm not here to play games. I'm here to kill the bugs." I glanced around, spotted six different species of aliens. "Are you the only survivors?"

A Gilian, with his face covered in eyes, blinked and said, "We got guns."

Typical Gilian. English was too hard to learn fully.

"Not all of us made it," the four-armed Marshall said. "Guns worked to keep the creatures away. We had to lock ourselves in our quarters and this dining area until we baited the creatures you were trying to kill."

"Cool story, bro," I said. "But what have you been doing since then? If those things in the bay aren't a threat, what are you doing to end the real threat?" God, I sounded so matter of fact. GAH! What the shit was going on? Better not be another growth spurt. Yeah, stupid joke. Hur-hur. Shut up.

The four-armed alien, whom I still couldn't place as a species, shrugged. "We are not equipped for combat."

"Really? Intergalactic Marshalls and you're not equipped for combat? What the loving shit *are* you equipped for?"

"We rotate, jackass," the Tulleev spouted. "This is like a vacation compared to our actual jobs. A few of us stop here, agree to help with security. Rest. And then onto our next criminal. Not like you'd understand, but there you go."

I chuckled. "Oh, I really like you. By the way, I'm a veteran Skull Dagger and Supreme Elite. I know full well about leave. Hell, I didn't carry anything more than six laser pistols and two plasma rifles on leave. Four guns less than I typically carried."

One of the other Marshalls, a lanky, gunslinger type, stepped forward. "I reckon military is different than the Marshalls. We're tactical, partner." He wore a broad brimmed hat and chewed on a thin, unlit cigar.

I snorted. "Settle down, Mr. Eastwood. I know you're 'different'." I turned to the others. "But you have me now. Once I exterminate the threat, get this fucker living again. And I mean the station. Jumpstart it. Whatever the shit you people do."

They all exchanged a glance.

A green, reptilian being shook its crocodilian head. "We ain't trained to run no station."

I blinked. "You ain't...okay, Sling Blade, step down. Any others out there willing to try?"

Of course, the Tulleev woman said, "For Bird, yes. I know some controls."

I nodded. "See, that's the sexiness I want. Who else?"

The four-armed alien raised two hands. "I can help."

I nodded. "Thank you, Happy Helpers. Bless your weird little hearts." I stepped back, so they could see me as an authority figure. I wasn't, but they didn't know that. And, if they did, they were too duh to realize it. "You two follow behind me. Stay at least fifty yards away at all times. Move in when the plasma blasts stop longer than two minutes."

The Tulleev opened her mouth to either ask a question or tell me to fuck off, but I said, "If there are too many bugs, get your asses back here and let me take care of the threat. But don't just sit and twiddle your thumbs, figure out an alternate plan if I fail."

The four-armed freak and the Tulleev nodded in tandem.

I glanced at the others. "Same with all you. Don't just fuck around here. There has to be escape pods somewhere, right? Use those noggins of yours. If all goes well, everything will be online soon." I gave the Tulleev and four-armed alien a nod. "Let's go fuck shit up."

***

We exited the cafeteria opposite the door I entered.

"The core is this way," the Tulleev said, hurrying ahead of me.

"Hey, pump the brakes, Roadrunner." I brushed by her. "Stay behind me. Give me directions as we go."

"You're kind of an ass," she said.

"Yeah, well, it's either me or sit in that tomb back there and rot."

That shut her up. But, of course, didn't stop my mouth from yammering. "What's your name anyway, you little bundle of angst?"

"Seri."

I nodded. "And you, Four-Arms?"

"Crown Royal, sir."

I blinked, stopped walking and spun around. "Crown...Royal? You fuckin' with me right now, Four-Arms?"

"No."

"She's from the Epilu moon," Seri said.

"Ah, the Junk Moon." I waved a hand while walking. "Sorry, Crown Royal. Don't mind me, I'm an alcoholic."

"An...alcoholic...?"

"Settle down back there, Crown," I spouted. "You're makin' me thirsty."

She fell silent. Probably not sure what the hell I was talking ab—

My suit lights caught the glimpse of silvery eyes down the corridor. I squinted, trying to determine if what I saw was just reflecting metal…or something else. The suit couldn't determine one or the other.

"Welp," I said. "Only one way to find out."

"What?" Seri asked behind me.

"Nothing. Back away," I said. "Keep low. Get those pistols ready."

Seri and Crown said nothing. Which was good. I hated explaining myself more than once.

A shriek echoed throughout the corridor. *That* definitely wasn't reflective metal.

I slapped the left plasma rifle on to the back magnetic plate and pointed the right plasma. Those silvery eyes blinked. I grinned.

"Here comes the boom, motherfucker."

I squeezed the trigger. Pale blue illuminated the darkness, revealing the owner of the silvery eyes. A slug-like creature covered in bony spikes slid toward me leaving a long slime trail behind. Its maw gaped open. Rows and rows of small, hooked teeth spiraled all the way to its throat.

It let go another loud shriek just before the first two rapid blasts obliterated its head in a spatter of dark green.

It plopped over, twitching.

"Hail to the New King, baby," I muttered and stomped by the dead thing. "C'mon, you two. Let's get this over with."

Honestly, I probably should have left them back in the cafeteria. Bringing them along only meant disaster. They were Marshalls. Relative badasses. They knew how to defend themselves and beat some ass, at least. Although, from what I saw, they weren't as badass as their reputation alluded. Intergalactic law enforcement was a far cry from the Military. Especially tactical specialist and the like.

And me…

Yeah. I should've left them where they would at least have a better chance of surviving.

Then again, what fun would that be?

By the look of 'em, they needed a little excitement in their lives.

I promised myself I wouldn't let them die.

"Right," Seri said as I approached a T-intersection. "Forty feet, there'll be a door on the left and a set of stairs going down."

I snorted. "Listen, lady. I don't go down on the first date. Caught a bad set of Raspis crabs doing that one night and swore to myself, *never* again, Clusterfuk. Ya wanna go down on a woman, you wait until the second date, because—"

"God," Seri interrupted. "You're the most insufferable asshole I've ever met."

I opened the door to the stairs and faced her. "Okay. Serious time, kiddos. Crown, watch our backs. Any movements, sounds, anything, you give a shout, got it?"

She nodded.

"Cereal. I'll need you to—"

"Seri."

"Don't interrupt me, young lady."

She rolled her bright, blue eyes. "Just spit it out."

I sighed. "Yeesh. Tough crowd. Yeah, Sera, you'll make sure both of you are behind me at least twenty yards. Shit hits the fan and looks hopeless, go back to the cafeteria."

"It's *Seri*, idiot, and what are you going to do for light? We can't see anything and if you're that far ahead we'd be running into everything."

Well, shit. That wasn't something I considered. How *were* they going to see? An idea surfaced through my swirling thoughts.

"Back lights," I said.

"Uh…what?" Seri frowned in the glow of my lights.

"Wait for it."

In my ear, the helm said, "Back lights, engaged."

I turned around and said, "Can ya see now?"

A pause. "Uh, yeah. I'm blind now. Thanks, dickhead."

"I'm a big ball of pretty lights," I mused.

"Mr. Clusterfuk," Crown said. "You seem to be a bit off kilter. Do you feel well?"

"Can it, sweet Canadian nectar!" I started forward. "I can be pretty too."

FOURTEEN

Seri remained close, sometimes bitching about the back lights, and guided me closer to the core.

For being a station infested with bugs, it was the poorest example of infestation I'd ever seen in all my years exterminating bugs with the Skull Daggers. Jeff was a lying bastard and I meant to ask him, personally, why he'd do me like that.

This was all just a little too easy…

The temp outside the suit increased a couple degrees. From seventy-two to seventy-four.

"How close are we?" I asked.

"It's straight ahead. Not far now."

I frowned. "I thought the real threat was near the core?"

"Yes," Crown spouted from the rear. "Our last signature images revealed a strong concentration near and at the core."

"Okay. So…shouldn't we be crawling with bugs right now?"

Neither Crown, nor Seri replied. Totally leaving me hanging. Dicks…

Before long, it was so bright, I didn't need any of the suit's lights on. I stopped and gaped at the massive, pulsating yellow orb floating in the center of a cavernous room. It was surrounded by platforms and pipes that stuck into it and snaked away into various parts of the station. Red squiggles surged over the core's yellow surface, stuttered, then sunk back into the giant ball of energy.

How it was still contained and hadn't exploded yet was beyond me. Without a stable environment, cores were known to not give a shit and obliterate everything within one hundred thousand miles.

That one, though, it still appeared to give a shit. Or, at least curious about it. But…

"Where's all the bugs?" I asked, mostly to myself.

"I…" Seri said. "I don't know. Maybe they went somewhere else?"

"Or maybe," I said, "you guys were just seeing the radiant energy of this sexy core in your images."

They stood on either side of me now. Because, fuck orders, right?

"No," Crown said. "There was movement in the images. Sporadic."

"Yeah?" I turned to her. "Who all saw those images?"

Her gaze dropped away from me and I couldn't help but chuckle.

"You're a liar, my little four-armed Canadian lush."

Her big, black eyes blinked. She looked at me. "I swear, sir, I saw movement."

I slapped the laser pistol out of her hand and tapped the tip of my arm blade under her chin. "Who paid you?"

"Clint," Seri said. "Crown has been in the Marshall's service for over sixty years. She's a highly decorated officer. Why would she lie?"

I grunted and turned away from them both. "Money changes people. No matter what species you are."

"I assure you, sir," Crown said. "I cannot lie."

I didn't look at her, nor did I acknowledge her claim. They all denied everything anyway. And that went for every species. Same as me, I guess. If I got called out every time for badmouthing locals…

I knew Crown was from the Junk Moon, but should I automatically call her a liar so soon?

No.

In a gullible world, one soaked in naivety though, I would almost believe her. Of course, I knew better.

"So," I said, "what was your plan, Crown Drunky Pants? Wait everyone out, plunder the place, turn everything back on and escape pod to the nearest planet? Then what? Disappear with all the loot until you need more? Am I getting warm?"

Crown blinked her buggy, black eyes.

"What are you talking about?" Seri asked. "Crown isn't a pirate."

"Sure she is. A lazy sleazy pirate, sure, but a pirate she is."

Seri snapped a glance at Crown. "You've been with the Marshalls for fifty years, though."

"I know. He's lying." Crown straightened. "Why would an Intergalactic Marshall—"

Seri lifted the laser pistol and pulled the trigger. In a flash, Crown's head exploded into a mess of smoldering gray. Most of it splattered all over the wall behind her, oozing down the metallic surface like honey.

I blinked.

Seri holstered the gun.

"I…I think I love you," I said.

"Shut up. You were right. Hate myself for not seeing it sooner."

"How'd you figure it out?"

She sighed and said, "Crown was supposed to be with the Marshalls for sixty years. I said fifty this last time. It was all the proof I needed when she didn't catch it."

"Because the older ones *always* keep track of their time served," I said.

"Exactly."

"Well, holy shit, I was right!"

She frowned. "You mean…you didn't really know for sure?"

I shrugged. "I figured you'd catch it eventually. I just needed to shine a light on it."

"Wait," Seri said, shoving me. "You were *guessing*?"

"Of course I was, Pretty Purple Girl. C'mon. Let's see about turning this big bastard on, eh?"

Seri was quiet for a few seconds, then said, "There seemed like more aliens aboard when everything went down. The loading bay could barely be half of them."

"Maybe you saw things wrong," I said. "I mean, I do that all the time in the fog of battle. Miscount, fall down, get up, shoot, miscount some more. Happens."

"No," she said. "Something feels off. Maybe we should wait and check things out before—"

"Oh, horse nuts. We're fine. Bet most of the bugs died out of starvation anyway." I stepped into a domed command center. "Let's get this rust heap running again. We'll set the escape pods for Upious and send for help from there."

"Upious?" She made a weird, disgusted face. "The number one illegal drug manufacturer of HOB Galaxy?"

I smiled. "Yaas. Good cash crop industry. Lovely species, really."

"No," she said. "Pick another planet."

I glanced over the control panel. "It's the closest and safest, there, Little Purple People Eater."

"Fine," she said, pushing me out of the way. "Give me a second. I killed the one person who really knew how to start up a space station."

"Way to go, lady," I spouted.

"Because *you* led me to believe she was a pirate!"

"Oh, pish-posh. Ya gonna start this beast up, or what?"

She sighed, though didn't say anything, and went about getting the station up and running. Or, at the very least, the escape pod area.

I stepped away from the command center and stared at the pulsating core. The helm's visor blocked any damaging light. Those red squiggles fluttered over its surface before disappearing again.

I hadn't witnessed many station cores in my time, but those I did…never were there red squiggles.

Something was wrong with the core. A virus, maybe? Or…

"A trap," I whispered to myself, eyes widening. I spun, stumbled into the command center dome. "We need to—"

"Warning," the AI of the station said. "Alien presence detected."

The floor trembled under my boots.

"What the hell?" Seri said, glancing at the floor.

"Yup. We need to move. Now." I swung her out of the command center and followed closely behind.

Shrieks and roars filled the air. An odd rip, like someone tearing a sheet of paper apart, cut through the other noises. Curious, I spared a glance over my shoulder. What appeared to be long, black, spider legs emerged from the core.

I faced forward. "Move those honey buns, lady."

"Maybe...if you...picked me up and carried me..." She said between breaths.

"Oh for fuck sake. Just run to that door."

"Ass...hole..."

"Listen here, my purple goddess. As much as I love viewing your assets, we have a bit of a situation here. I suggest you kinda follow my lead." I paused. "Or I'll feed you to whatever just crawled out of the core."

"I...wasn't...argu—"

"Yeah, yeah. Get movin' wheezy."

Luckily, the door I chose was of the rare hinged vintages. I opened it for Seri, swung her into the darkness beyond, and said, "Get back to the cafeteria. Figure out a way off this station."

I slammed the door before she could yell at me and faced the core. The light in the cavernous area flickered while the core waxed and waned.

While monsters crawled out of it.

It wasn't a core anymore. It was a goddamn portal. How that all came about, shit, I dunno. All I knew was one thing...

I refreshed the plasma canisters (two more left) and narrowed my gaze at the creatures still spilling out the core, portal...whatever.

"It's Clusterfuk time."

I ran at them. Large monsters I never saw before, nor heard of. Creatures with spindly black widow legs and a dragon-like body. All shiny black scales, snapping maws filled with curved teeth, and lashing, spiky tails. White smoke curled upward in long tendrils out their flaring nostrils. Red eyes flashed while their numbers grew.

I couldn't even count them all.

They didn't notice me yet. Too busy shaking off whatever portal jetlag they had going on, probably.

Just the way I liked it.

About twenty yards from the bastards, I jumped and activated the antigravity boots. The boost sent me almost one hundred feet in the air.

Or, somewhere around there. Okay, I didn't know. But it could've been one hundred feet. Shut up.

Once above them, I cut the antigravity and divebombed the monstrosities.

Stupid, sure, but I lived for that shit.

"Surprise, motherfuckers," I shouted and lit the sons of bitches up.

Silvery blood sprayed the air. Screams rose to shrill shrieks.

I didn't know if I killed any of them on my descent, nor did I care. I shifted my position at the last second and slammed onto a random, scaly back hard enough to hear it break upon impact. Even over all the surprised shrieking. The creature buckled under me, thudded to the floor. I stormed along the shattered spine and blew the fucker's head off.

A tail smacked into me from out the maelstrom. I flew backward until I crashed into another monster. It reared, spidery legs flicking sporadically at the air. The dragon maw opened, a bright, fiery ball building in its throat.

My eyes widened. Holy shitnuggets. They breathed fire, like actual dragons? Wait, dragons weren't real. Unless they always existed in a different dimension and somehow found themselves on Earth through some rift or another every now and then. Which, I guess, made sense considering all the stories. Or maybe not. Shit, I didn't know.

Anyway, I pummeled the bastard's head with plasma blasts until it exploded in a fireball. Seared chunks of brain, muscle and bone rained down, clinking off my suit.

They weren't bugs or alien masterminds, exactly, but interdimensional beings…? Shit, I didn't know. Tons of planets and moons scattered all six known galaxies, so…

A black spider's leg swung and struck me hard enough in the head to make me stumble and the helm buzz a bit. Another creature swept my legs out from under me and before I knew it, I gaped up at the smoldering nostrils and red eyes of a monster fully intent on eating me. Or, at the very least, injuring me so bad I'd no longer be a threat.

"Oh, eat warty cocks, dickshit," I said and sent a ton of rounds into its ugly-ass head, draining most of both canisters. "Fuck." I glared at the headless dead thing. "Worth it."

Silvery blood splattered everything. Mostly the floor. My suit had to adjust its balance while I slipped and slid through the mess.

WARNING: EXTERIOR ON FIRE.

I stopped. Lifted an arm, noted the flames and dropped it.

"What the *shit*?" I spun, finding the ugly shitplunger that turned me into a walking barbeque.

A deep growl rumbled in its throat. White smoke snaked out of its nostrils. Its red eyes narrowed to slits.

"Ohhh, you're a—"

Something struck me from the side, sending me flying. The suit beeped, telling me its shields were now at twenty percent.

I slammed into the command center, landing on the control panels. Sparks bloomed like fireworks.

Red, hot rage leaked through my brain. "Mother*fucker*."

I stormed out of the busted command center, checked the energy levels of the plasma canisters. Both rested at an easy forty percent. I had two more and dozens of the ugly wankers.

Wankers? Goddamn it, Australia!

Soft clicking. Low growls. A long hiss.

I blinked, turning in a lazy circle.

"Well, you clever interdimensional fuckwads," I said.

They surrounded me. Like, completely. There wasn't a hole between them. They were all different in appearance, yet similar. That one had horns poking out of its face. The one next to it was smaller than the others. Differences equaled similarities. Not like bugs, which were more similar than different in every case I came across. Might as well have been legions of clones.

But the creatures surrounding me, while they slowly closed in, were individuals working as a unit. Like a Marine platoon. Calculated. Something I really hadn't faced before. I mean, some bugs and alien forces could be individual and a working unit at the same time, but it was fairly rare.

Nothing like what I currently found myself pitted against.

Shield was at twenty percent.

Only two plasma canisters left.

Called for some serious precision if I wanted to have enough ammo to waste them all.

A few of the monsters opened their toothy maws, revealing balls of fire roiling at the back of their throats.

They closed in. Some crawled over small buildings I assumed were for storage, while others crept and slithered and scuttled between obstacles. Spiderlike. Graceful, yet meticulous. Were dragon spiders even a thing? In all my twenty-three years of military experience…I neither saw, nor heard of such monstrosities.

How did you fight something that wasn't supposed to exist?

Well…easy answer was blow them to smoldering bits. Which posed an even harder answer: How the hell did you kill them all when you had a severe shortage of ammo?

Only thirty yards away, the monsters closed the gap between us.

I guess I could just lay down and let them kill me. I could…

But what fun would that be?

I grinned. "Let's rock, you scaly cunts."

I turned in a slow circle, aiming my plasma rifles. The suit did its thing, locking in and straightening my arms. Theoretically, every shot should be a headshot.

Sometimes, the suit could be just a tad off.

They sprinted toward me. A closing mass of teeth and scuttling legs and building fiery breath.

I squeezed the triggers. Bright blue blasts pummeled into dragon head after dragon head and—

What the hell was that?

Snaking out from under the creatures came more monsters. These resembled massive centipedes with a serpent's head. All fangs and drippy venom.

"You gotta be fucking kidding me," I said and stopped turning, fingers letting up on the triggers.

Dozens of the new creatures scurried my way. Longer than a goddamn school bus.

"Antigravity, engage," I said and jumped.

And not a moment too soon. They all collided into each other below me. Actually attacking each other. I watched one of the centipede things burrow into a spider dragon thing and burst out its maw in a fount of silvery blood.

So gross.

I jumped again, getting as high as I could.

When I looked down again, though…

"Bugger me."

They were piling on top of each other like insects. Ants. Whatever. Building up and up. Higher and higher.

Never in all my life had I witnessed something like that. Even in bugs. These things worked together, though not collectively. They appeared to compromise while they built their living tower to get to me. I couldn't help but watch, heart thrumming, while they crawled over others and piled on.

"Oh," I said, "this is fuckin' nuts."

I shifted, aimed at the base of the tower, and let'em have it. I took it out in not time, toppling their tower. Silver blood splashed.

It was fantastic.

They blew fire up at me, not at all coming close. Soon enough, they began to rebuild their living tower again. Because, of course they did. Bastards.

I checked the percentage of the canisters. Equal ten percent.

Lovely.

I'd been in such situations before, but never at such a magnitude with so many creatures to deal with and so little ammo. Totally ridiculous.

Hated myself for not grabbing more canisters. Eh, but could you do, right?

A bead of sweat trickled down my nose. The suit was a sauna most of the time, but right then…it felt more like an oven set at three hundred and fifty degrees. I was baking to death. Not really, but it felt like it. Totally redonkulous.

I couldn't even count how many there were, but I figured somewhere in the hundreds.

And…I'm one dude in a suit with ten percent shield. Once that shield was gone, it would be pretty much game over, man.

An expert would say I needed a plan. They would have a strategy all worked out in minutes. Me…it was blast and tear.

If it was my time, then so be it.

"Antigravity off."

The boots disengaged and plummeted toward the enemy.

I divebombed the bastards, pointed the plasma rifles, and let loose. Some blood splattered one of the nearby spider dragons' face.

"Yeah, baby, that's the money shot," I shouted.

In a matter of a couple of seconds (and a few monsters slaughtered) I landed hard on top of one of the centipede things. It reared, made an odd yowl, and tried to double back on itself to get me.

I leaped, fired two rounds into the gaping serpent's mouth. To my surprise, red exploded in the air. Red blood, typically, was associated with humans or Earth species. Very rare to find something not of Earth bleed red. And yet, there we were…

Dozens of sharp cries sliced through the growling and hissing. And holy nutballs, they sounded pissed. The other centipede things. I'd put money on it. I just killed one of their family members and now, instead of coming after me just to kill me…they wanted revenge. Which meant, they probably wouldn't kill me outright and let me suffer for a while.

The centipede things appeared to be connected by some biological link. Like bees, if I remembered right. Once you killed a bee, it released a signal or pheromones, whatever. It told the rest of the hive one of their own had just been splattered. The rest of the hive would go batshit and attack everything until the threat was dead or gone.

Apparently, the centipede things were bees.

Lovely.

The spider dragons scuttled back and forth as the serpent centipedes made their way out of the horde at me.

I ejected the spent canisters, slapped the fresh ones in, and blew out a slow breath.

FIFTEEN

They spilled out from between the spider dragons like a scuttling tsunami with teeth.

"Antigravit—"

A tail crashed into my side, sending me cartwheeling. I plopped onto my back and glared at the visor. The shields were now at fifteen percent.

"Goddamn it," I said.

The moment I stood, one of the centipedes pummeled into me. Before I knew it, I was chest deep in its snake-like mouth.

"Look, dude," I said. "I don't kiss on the first date."

I slammed the muzzle of my plasma rifle against the creature from the outside, hoped I didn't blow myself to kibble, and fired.

I stumbled backward, red blood covering my visor. Suddenly my arms were pinned to my sides. The suit beeped. A warning on the visor told me the intakes were in danger of being clogged.

What the shit?

I shuffled, trying to figure out what the hell was going on. I knew the creature was dead, so…what now? Why were my damn arms pinned? Why couldn't I see? Even with the blood I should be able to…

That was when I looked up through the neck-hole and two things struck me at once like a fuckin' hammer and anvil combo.

I was still in the serpent's head and stumbling around like a dotard, and…the other creatures were staring at me like I was some kind of escaped mental patient. I swear to god, if they cock an eyebrow…

Okay, so, I'm shuffling around in a massive serpent's head like an idiot and surrounded by the enemy, whom, I was pretty sure, were laughing on the inside. Because, assholes gonna asshole.

I went to try and break out of the head, but, of course, it was a snake. It was flexible so it could swallow prey whole. Every attempt to rip and tear ended in wasted energy.

WARNING: INTAKE # 2 CLOGGED.

Well, now, wasn't that just lovely?

There was only one way to get out the weird situation I found myself in.

I plopped to the floor and kinda flopped around until I slipped out of the head. The curved fangs screeched against the suit, but other than that, all good.

Freedom at last!

Still, I could barely see through all the blood. And the suit decided right then to unclog intake number two. It did the whole weird pressure thing until the clog was expelled. I moved around, semi-blind. I could see things, just not very clearly. Which sucked fuzzy donkey balls. If I ever made it out alive, I was gonna demand the Elite suit be updated to involve visor cleaning and—

DO YOU WISH TO CLEAN HELMET VISOR?

I blinked at the words scrolling before my eyes. How come nobody told me about—

"Uh, yeah."

VISOR CLEANING ENGAGED.

The blood bubbled crazily until it finally slipped away. The visor was completely clean.

"Guess next time I should read the instruction manual," I said to myself.

They loomed over me. All reared up like the partial serpents they were. Their forked tongues flickered the air. Amber eyes revealed not an iota of emotion. Why weren't they attacking? Surely, while waiting for the clog to be blown out and the visor to be cleaned, they could've torn me apart if they wanted to.

Instead, they stared at me. They didn't move. Shit, they didn't even make a sound.

Behind the loose circle, the spider dragon creatures also watched.

My gods of chunky peanut butter, I felt like I was on some sleazy webcam, or something.

Well, they're not getting the jackoff show. Nope. Fuckers wanted a show they should've paid instead of, ya know, trying to eat me and shit.

"So," I said, "how y'all doin'? Good? Look, I didn't mean to get your friend's head stuck on me. That shit was messed up but I—"

They all struck at once.

"Oh! Struck a nerve." I blasted most of their heads off and about commanded the suit to antigravity when one of the slimy bastards coiled around me.

Once more, I found my arms pinned to my sides. Once more…helpless. If there was anything I truly hated, feeling helpless was it.

WARNING: INCREASING PRESSURE.

I glared at the words scrolling across my visor and wanted to punch them. I mean, *duh*. I was in the coils of a fuckin' snakepede for shit sake. Of *course* I was being crushed to death, stupid visor!

Fuck it.

I dropped the right plasma rifle and curled my hand into a tight fist. The retractable blade shot out. It must've hurt the creature because it squealed like a scared pig. The hold on me loosened and I took advantage of it.

With an upward slash, I cut through the creature's body. Weird, white pustules beaded outside the sliced skin. The cut began to close. Wait, was it healing?

I blinked. A sudden, frightening image popped into my noggin.

The night my parents were killed. I didn't really capture much about the creature's actual identity. All I recalled about it were teeth and how fast it moved. But, right then, I remembered something more. The way it scuttled and slithered through the house. The reptilian head...

My eyes widened while everything clicked together.

It wasn't just a bug that killed my parents, but the snakepedes. My mind must've blocked a lot of the details out. But now...

I snapped back to reality, knowing what really killed my parents. What gave me weird healing abilities. It wasn't just some rogue bug. It was the creatures I faced right then. The ones from, not another planet, but dimension.

With such a revelation, white hot rage surged through me. It wasn't the creature that killed my family, but *its* kin. And *they* wanted vengeance for killing one of their own (or rather, two) and I wanted vengeance for the slaughter of my family.

I didn't know where it came from, the one that killed my parents and gave me the healing ability. Either it accidentally slipped through some rift, or just a violent rouge. Either way, I blew its head to bits with Dad's laser scatter gun. Didn't matter. All I knew, right then, was how I hated their very existence.

Every. Last. One.

The cut healed completely. The snakepede shrieked.

"Antigravity, engage!"

I jumped into the air, barely avoiding more than a couple of the creatures' snapping maws. The spiderdragons spat fire at me. They roared. They scuttled about, jumping at me and missing while I rose closer and closer to the ceiling. Once more, they began piling on top of each other.

The one I cut open, the one that healed, remained where I left it. Its amber eyes narrowed. On the floor beside it rested my other plasma rifle.

Goddamn it.

"Fuck you," I said to the one glowering at me. "Antigravity, disengage."

I shot downward, plasma rifle lit. The son of a bitch dodged every blast and snaked into the crowd.

Shit. Lost him.

"Antigravity pulse, engage," I said and came to a jolting halt a few feet over the floor, nearly losing whatever floated around in my stomach at the same time.

In a second, I pulsed inches above the floor. "Antigravity pulse, disengage." I thumped to the floor, opened my fist to draw the blade back into the suit's arm, and grabbed my fallen rifle.

I didn't have time for anything else.

They swarmed over me before I could move, blotting out the glow from the pulsating core turned rift. Or whatever the hell it was.

"You greasy cockshits," I shouted and squeezed the rifle triggers.

WARNING: SHIELD 5%.

That shit pissed me off even more. Blood splashed over me. I didn't stop shooting. I couldn't stop. Battle fog obscured everything. I just didn't care. Nothing mattered but ripping and shredding and pulverizing. Beating the ugly bastards into twitchy pulps. Everything was blood and sporadic blue flashes, and I just didn't give a fuck anymore.

My right plasma had sixty percent energy and draining. The left edged down into the seventy percent region.

Finally, I burst out of the grotesque doggy pile they put me in. Blood. Red and silver, both sprayed the air and rained over me. My boots splashed through all the blood as I hurried away from all the madness.

Soon, I stopped, realizing nothing was trying to kill me.

I turned around and blinked at the small mountain of dead things. Some were trying to heal and failing. Headshots were the ticket with the snakepedes. A thing I knew from past experience. They couldn't heal very well, if at all, when their head was blown to bits. Not all of them were the snakepedes, either. A few spiderdragons were tossed in the bloody mix too. I turned, finding the rest of the spiderdragons gaping at the gory pile I created.

Heh. I slinked away, taking advantage in the lull of attention. There weren't as many as before, though enough to tear me apart. I'd say somewhere in the hundreds.

Carefully, I wound myself through the stunned stillness. I needed to get to a better advantage point once they broke out of whatever silly fugue they were frozen in. I needed to be ready to pick each one off, before all the energy in the canisters were spent. Which meant...sniper action.

"Antigravity, engage." I leaped toward the ceiling until I found a nice maintenance platform to stand on. It was small and narrow and obviously meant to check on that section's integrity, but it'd do.

All I needed was to have the high ground. They could pile up all they wanted. So long as I could take them out one at a time until only a few remained…then so be it. And that was my plan. Do the sniper thing until only a few scurried about. I didn't know if I killed all the snakepedes, nor did I care.

I had the motherfuckin' high ground.

It didn't take them long to snap back to reality. When they did, another full minute or two lapsed before they realized where I was. Before that, I blew the heads off at least ten spiderdragons within that minute.

Well, hell, apparently, I wasn't too bad at the sniper thing.

I went to aim on another creature, when a shriek rose directly above me.

"Jesus jumpin' on a fuckin' tortoise, *really*?" I glanced up to find one of the snakepedes, mouth open. Its legs gradually released from the ceiling, lowering itself.

It gave a crackly hiss.

"You're still living?" I said just before it struck and I jammed a plasma rifle into its mouth.

Boom.

Its head exploded into a splatter of red and teeth.

"Not anymore mate." I snorted and went about doing the sniping thing when a series of crackles drew my attention back to the ceiling.

Blood poured out the headless creature, but that wasn't what made the noises. No, it was…

The last few legs snapped free of the ceiling and the giant, headless, snakepede crashed down on top of me.

Once more in darkness, I sighed. "I really hate these things…" I triggered the arm blade and sliced my way through the body until I stood in the mediocre light of the core/ rift thingy.

I was just getting ready to shove the headless corpse off the landing when something popped under me. Not like a gunshot. More metallic. It had a twang to it I didn't like at all. I pushed harder, using the suit's extra strength to get most of the bastard over the edge—

A few more pops, and the landing began to sway.

"Shit," I said, still pushing.

It wasn't cables snapping, but bolts. At least I thought they were bolts. Didn't matter. The landing couldn't handle the added weight of the snakepede. Soon it'd…

A sharp clank and there we went. My headless snakepede friend and I, plummeting toward the floor and the eager toothy, fiery mouths of the spiderdragons.

"Antigravity, engage," I shouted and shot upward, narrowly avoiding the landing.

I switched to antigrav pulses just a few feet under the ceiling of pipes and cords. It took a lot of pipes and cords to keep a station running smoothly. Felt sorry for the poor bastards that had to run and piece it all together. Bots did most of the hard labor, but it took a human's creativity and ingenuity to work around problems nine times out of ten.

The landing managed to kill a couple of spiderdragons for me. The others ate the headless snakepede. Well, most of the others. A few watched me very carefully. Calculating my movements. Those, I assumed, were the elders of the bunch. I roughly counted two dozen of the creatures left. Probably more, maybe less.

One plasma canister read: 30%.

The other read: 51%.

If I aimed perfectly every time, killing them all shouldn't be a problem. But if I missed, just once, yeah, might as well hang up the hat and call it a day. Not that I'd really do that, but, ya know…

So, floating in the air, I aimed my lowest percentage plasma at one of the elders glaring at me.

"Night, night, motherfucker," I said and squeezed the trigger.

Boom went the misshapen dragon head in a spatter of silver.

I took out all six of the bastards watching me before the canister read: 10%. One more blast, and that gun was gone. I took aim on the biggest, ugliest bastard, and blew its head off. I dropped the spent gun, lifted the other, and blew the heads off a few others until my final plasma canister dropped to twenty percent.

By the time the rifle canister was spent, I'd killed over sixty monsters while they spat fire at me. If that didn't earn me a Medal of Honor, I didn't know what would. I mean, c'*mon*. Regardless, I still had about thirty more to go.

Twenty percent plasma…one hundred percent badass.

Fuck yeah.

"Antigravity, disengage," I said and dropped like a boulder.

I took out a few before pulse landing on the soupy floor. Red and silver mingled and swirled. If I didn't know it was blood, I would almost be cool looking. The blood pooled just over the tops of my boots. And, considering how huge the core bay was, yeah, that's a lot of fuckin' blood, people.

They struck all at once and with a ferocity the others hadn't shown. Fire and scuttling, black spider legs, maws lined with teeth snapping at me. That's all I knew. With a clench of my fist, I triggered the arm blade and swept it at all those teeth and red eyes, slicing snouts clean off and sheering gobs of meat from their faces.

"Back off, twatwaffles," I said and hacked my way through spider legs and lashing tails.

WARNING: SUIT ON FIRE.

Yeah, I figured that would happen.

WARNING: SHIELDS AT 3%.

That…I didn't figure on. Christ, they were digging at me from every direction. Fire. Teeth. Claws. Tails. Once the shields fell, they'd be damaging the suit. It was a tough armor but would require me to be smart and shit. Otherwise it'd break down and they'd peel me open like one of those old sardine cans. No more of the balls to the wall hack'em up, boom-boom greatness I loved.

I stumbled out of the madness at three percent shields.

Six of the bastards lay away from the others, mewling from the wounds my blade inflicted. I smiled. Good. Let'em hurt a while. As for the rest…

Yeah, they were all looming over me. Smoke squiggled from their flaring nostrils.

At least twenty of them.

I blasted about eight with the plasma before the canister was spent. Problem was my position. They were towering sons of bitches, while I was just little ol' me. My angle was all wrong. I blasted through bellies and chests until finally getting to the head. Ammo wasted, pretty much.

A heavy sigh blew out of me. I dropped the plasma rifle, stepping away while the fifteen or so spiderdragons came at me.

I was fucked. No way around it. Because…

"No," I said. "Wait."

Every Elite suit had a backup shield. Nothing big. Maybe fifty percent. Still, it was something. On the other hand, it took away from other strengths the suit had. Like the antigravity thing and strength thing.

I backed away while they advanced. I nodded, knowing what needed to be done.

I side-stepped right as one of them scurried too close and hacked four spider legs in half before the next creature came for me. I swung around, taking the heavy blow to the shoulder in order to uppercut the jackass through the mouth up into its stupid brain.

The spiderdragon slumped. I yanked the blade out and let the bastard fall. I swung and caught the next monster in mid-claw. Literally. My nearly three-foot blade stabbed through its claw, stopping it from decapitating me.

I roared, shoving the blade forward. It sliced the claw right down the middle. The spiderdragon yowled.

I patted its steaming, quivering muzzle. "Hurts me more than you, bruh."

It reared, maw open and ready to clamp down over me.

Moving as fast as the suit would enhance, I wacked half its lower jaw off and plunged the blade into the side of its head. Its red eyes went weird. Like, the left side, where the blade sank in, the eyeball looked at me. The right however, lolled, nesting itself in the far-right side of the socket. As far away as it could get from the blade, in other words. Probably, but more like muscles and tendons relaxing. I yanked the blade out and the creature collapsed at my boots.

Before my brain caught up, I was swept up into a toothy maw and being carried toward the remaining spiderdragons. The jaws clamped on so tightly my visor flickered with a pressure warning.

My shield flicked from three to two percent.

A new development: I felt those jaws. The suit's chest plate groaned. Gradually, dents appeared at the point of every tooth.

One percent shield.

"Goddamn it."

I yanked the arm with the blade, which flailed outside of the mouth, inward, breaking through some teeth.

The monster roared. Fire lit the back of its throat.

"Oh, shut up." I plunged the blade into the roof of its mouth.

A burst of fire shot me out of its mouth. I landed hard on my side and slid through all the blood for a while. I stood, wondering just how the shit the shield remained at one percent, and turned.

Eight spiderdragons glowered down at me. Like, barely twenty feet away.

"Oh," I said. "Hey, guys! We still on for poker tonight?"

They all roared at me.

I grunted. "Rude."

They scrambled toward me.

I darted to the side, using quick action functions to jump and dodge their attacks. Mainly, I needed to avoid catching fire. That shit was fucked up, yo.

I sprinted at one of the bastards, dropped to my knees, slid through the blood, and swept the arm blade in a heavy arc. I spun, still on my knees, still sliding and watched the spiderdragon's abdomen split and spread. A loop of gray intestine slipped out. The creature staggered, black widow legs quivering. Blood drizzled from the open wound.

As much as I wanted to revel in the death of the creature, the rest of its kin came after me. All fire and madness. I shot to the left and activated antigravity. With a jump, I rose above the monsters.

I didn't have a gun, so, improv, baby. All the best comedians did it. Also, the greatest warriors. Because, damn it, that's how we rolled. I could go antigravity and pick them off that way, but that would drain my shield some. Not much, but enough. A simple tail lash would break the shield. As it was, at a strong one percent, it could take a good strong hit from something. If depleted by fire though, a simple tail lash would probably break the suit.

It didn't matter how strong a suit was. If it got hammered by large monsters repeatedly, like anything, it'd wear down quickly. And never mind how I'd be pounded into yesterday's potato salad inside the damn thing.

I needed a different tactic…

SIXTEEN

The similarities between alien bugs and the ugly-ass spiderdragons were close. They swarmed, kinda. They never stopped. They made themselves a numerous force. Yet, they thought for themselves. Kinda.

Well, shit, look at that scaly shitcanoe over there, for instance. It eyed me from where it stood, near the core. Head all lowered, eyes glowing. Its upper muzzle curled a bit to reveal a few sharp teeth. It was pissed. Like, truly pissed. It wanted vengeance on my bloody ass. It purposely separated itself from the others.

Now, take a gander at the six scuttling fools no more than thirty yards from me while I climbed to the top of a small warehouse-like building. Totally collective. Overwhelm, destroy.

So weird.

Anyway, I climbed onto the top of the building and wished I had a gun. Even a lousy laser pistol would do. I could pick'em off quickly from where I stood. I held up the arm blade, shook my head, sighed, and lowered it again.

"Welp," I said. "Y'all like sushi. Wait, what's raw, cut up dragon meat called? Dragshi? Fuck yeah. Gimme that dragshi!"

They pummeled into the building, clawing their way up walls.

And thus, so far, my new tactic worked.

High ground, kids. Always get the high ground.

The first gnarly head popped over the edge of the flat roof. I buried my arm blade into its eye. Pink goo spurted around the blade and oozed off its shrieking, scaly face. Before it could spit fire at me, I slit its throat and shoved it off my roof. Its body twisted a bit, spider legs flailing, before it slammed onto the metal floor. Something green leaked from under its head. Flames crackled around the cut in its throat. The monster didn't move.

I turned, finding two more heads peeking over and one almost completely on the roof.

"You sneaky fucknut," I said and ran at the thing about to climb fully on.

I leaped, slashed the blade and took out three of its spider legs. It yowled, scrabbling to find a way to stay on the roof. I slammed the blade up through its lower jaw and into its beady brain.

I yanked it closer to me. "Nothing fucks with the Clusterfuk, asshole." I booted the ugly bastard off the roof and swung to the others.

Three more (well, four, including Mr. Broody-ass over by the core) and all three were pretty much on the roof.

Ugh, I talked too much sometimes. Or something. Whatever. Shut up.

"Okay," I said, mostly to myself. "Assholes gonna asshole."

I sprinted at them, caught one not quite onto the roof first. Severed a couple of legs. It squealed. No time to mess with that asshole, though. I focused on the other two. Both of them opened their maws. Fire crackled in their throats. Cowards, with their fire breath, and shit.

I needed to take a chance.

"Antigravity, engage."

I jumped above the monsters before they made me the main course of their barbecue, more or less. I jumped high above them, not really wanting to disengage the antigravity, but needing to. It drained the shields too much if I floated around trying to avoid being slaughtered.

Ah, but that wasn't the Clusterfuk way. The Clusterfuk was about action and ripping apart his enemies. The Clusterfuk wasn't one to let people down.

Aaand…why was I thinking of myself in the third person?

#clustercrackers

I disengaged the antigravity and dropped onto the back of the nearest spiderdragon.

"Okay, guys," I said, "it's been a real hoot'n all but…" I sliced the monster's head off. A fount of silvery blood erupted into the air.

The other two chomped at me. Flames burst through their teeth. Long, black tongues flailed. I leaped from the twitching mound of headless flesh and landed on one of the snapping dragonheads, driving it to the floor. Something cracked under my boot and I hoped it was the bastard's skull. The way it shoved me aside, though, I probably just broke a stupid tooth or something.

I stumbled, suit correcting the imbalance, and narrowly missed a scaly tail to the face. I crouched and sliced a large section of the tail off. Silver blood splattered all over me.

"Ew." I flapped my arms and hands, sending strings of the blood in every direction. I glared at the bastard with a partial tail. "Dude, I told you I wasn't into cumshots. I mean, goddamn, *really*?"

I flapped my arms and hands some more. "So gross."

While Half-Tail rolled around, howling and the other one just kind of glared at me, I snuck away to figure out my next move. Surprisingly, the one glaring at me didn't attack.

I glanced toward the core, but the monster must've moved. Where the ugly assface wandered off to, I didn't know. Creepy son of a bitch. I dashed around the warehouse building, regrouping my thoughts. Usually, I was pretty fuckin' impulsive, but the spiderdragons were different. I couldn't just slash and blast through'em all. The spiderdragons had a bit more brains than I was used to.

Did I tell anyone lately that I had to piss? Because, seriously…it was like bladder overload up in there. A sloshing bag of urine equaled me. I mean, I could just, kinda let it leak out. It'd reek in the suit, but so worth it. Better than rupturing something, right?

Right.

Fuck it.

Taking the suit off would mean suicide with the remaining spiderdragons creeping about, so…I peed in the suit.

You had to do what you had to do during battles.

Wasn't the first time I pissed in a suit or mech, anyway.

A dragon's head slipped around the far corner. I stopped. The heat of the pee already cooling. There were times in every life when a person hated themselves for one thing or another. Peeing in my suit was not one of those. Take that, sanitary codes!

Not the one that watched me carefully near the core. The one which had disappeared. Nope. It was the one that glared at me. Not in a very calculating way, but close enough, before I darted around the building.

The spiderdragon scuttled fully around the corner. It loomed over me, drool stringing from its horny lower jaw.

Snort. Horny.

Ahem, anyway, I went to stab the big bastard in the chest, but it scuttled away. Oh, it was a quick one. A deep growl rumbled in its throat. Small flames flickered through its teeth. We did a weird dosey-doe thing before it couldn't take anymore and spat a jet of fire at me. I dodged the fire, jumped and buried the arm blade deep in its chest.

It screamed like no other. I mean, damn…

Its softer underbelly gave way under my sharp blade and it slipped through lightly scaled, gray flesh, cutting it from mid-chest to the upper stomach region. Organs unfurled and spilled out. I backed away, avoiding the wave of blood and organs. Barely. Before I could move, however, it shot me with a fire burst.

WARNING: SUIT IS ON FIRE.

"Motherfucker," I roared, jumped, and cut the ugly whore's head off.

WARNING: SUIT HAS 0 SHIELD.

I gave the headless, eviscerated body a kick. "Thanks a lot, assnugget."

And so, I became a walking tin can. Wouldn't take much to fuck my world up. One more of those dragon wannabes hid out. It appeared way smarter than its kin. Like, mastermind smart. Or close. Okay, probably not. Whatever.

Where'd the fuckwad go, anyway?

I stepped away from the building, setting my suit visor to scan for movement, body heat, anything. As I walked around, even toward the core, nothing popped up. But it was there. I felt it. Working in the fields I became famous for I recognized the feel. The son of a bitch was cunning. Sneaky. It watched me closely while I sank a blade into the spiderdragon with the partial tail, even if I couldn't see it. It watched while I slowly made my way toward the core. The visor blinked: 0% Shields, and that was it. Not movement detection.

Nothing.

Maybe my feels were off, and the cunt scuttled along back to its real dimension. That would be alright.

I didn't ever worry about dying and had no idea why it worried me right then, but…shit, it did. And it pissed me off that it did. Pissed me right the fuck off. I worked better when I just didn't care about anything but ripping the enemy apart. What the shit was wrong with me?

A few feet from the pulsating core, I stopped and gave the area around me a good scan.

Nothing.

A low thrum came from the core. The red squiggles snaked across the surface. That was it. The visor didn't even pick up signs of life.

I waited a few minutes, scanning and watching. More nothing.

Eventually, I relaxed a bit, chuckled to myself and said, "Gettin' paranoid, man." I stepped away from the core. Now, I needed to get the others off the station and set the fuckin' thing up to explo—

A shrill whine filled my hearing. So shrill, I nearly tore my damn helmet off.

"Gah! What the—"

"Greetings, Mr. Clusterfuk," a jovial voice spat in my ears. One I didn't recognize at first.

When I didn't say anything, the over the top happy voice said, "I know you're alive. I know you can hear me. I know you're at the core. Now, I need to give you the final objective. And it's the most important."

I figured out the voice eventually. "Get bent, Jeff. There's nothing here you need."

"I want the Ethinian crystal that powers the core," Jeff (AKA the Employer) said. "Bring it to me, and you will be rewarded handsomely."

"Uh-huh," I said. "And what about the people still alive here?"

"What about them?"

I snorted. "Well, I can't just leave'em here…"

"Sure, you can. I'm not paying you to rescue survivors. I'm paying you to eliminate the initial threat and bring me the Ethinian crystal. That's it."

"Well, shit, maybe ya should've told me about this fuckin' crystal before? I'll get it, but I'll be coming home with a few extra folks."

"If you bring anyone else back with you, Mr. Clusterfuk, I can assure you your efforts will be in vain."

I frowned. "The hell does that mean?"

"It means," Jeff said, "I will not pay you and collect the crystal anyway. Then, I'll have you and whoever you drag along from that decrepit station executed."

I snorted. "Oh…my god. Dude! You're one of those old cliché villain types! So cute with your little twist just now. I *knew* there was something utterly douchey about you."

"Bring me the crystal, Clusterfuk, or…else."

I burst out laughing. Couldn't help it. Once it subsided, I said, "You…you…*really*? 'Or else.'" I laughed some more. "I can't believe you really threw that out there. I mean, you do realize what you're doing right?"

He paused for so long I figured he just hung up. But—

"Listen to me, you arrogant tripe. There's more at work here than you can possibly imagine. The rules are simple. Try not to let all the burrito and porn clog your brain. Bring me the crystal. I pay you. We go our separate ways. If you—"

"Listen, I'll have you know my burrito fetish is perfectly normal. I—"

A sharp click filled my hearing.

"Jeff?"

Nothing.

"Ah, c'mon, Jeffy!"

I chuckled, shook my head and continued searching for the final spiderdragon.

SEVENTEEN

I stopped searching and flapped my arms in exasperation. "Really, guy? Where the shit did you go? Olly olly oxen-free! Come on out, cuntburger."

Aaaand, nothing.

I literally searched the entire damn core room. Nothing but blood and corpses. So, where…

A loud squeal drew my attention up to a nearby landing. A door opened and…

"Jesus Christ doin' the Electric Slide," I shouted. "Don't *do* that!"

Seri glanced around all wide-eyed. "Y-You did all this?"

I sighed. "Well, duh. Who else?"

She shook her head. "How?"

"Darlin', if I tell ya, I'll have to kill ya."

"But, you're just one—*oh*!"

I nodded. "I know. I know. I have that effect on people. Pretty much an instant orgasm from the—"

"Behind you!"

I spun and found myself gaping up at the elusive spiderdragon. Its muzzle peeled back, revealing long, curved teeth. Smoke curled from its nostrils. Its red eyes narrowed on me. A deep growl rumbled somewhere in its narrow chest.

Fuck it.

"Hey," I shouted. "It's about fuckin' time, man! Where've you been? How's Mom? Still eating the dead flies on the windowsill?"

It struck without warning. So fast, I was only able to move the slightest. And just enough. Instead of its teeth, the side of its head thumped me aside. I stumbled, recovered and about commanded the suit to go antigravity when I remembered I didn't have that luxury anymore. All the power needed was to be put into strength and speed. No special toys.

There wasn't any time to recover before I narrowly dodged its tail and a burst of fire. It struck me with a spidery leg and I tumbled away.

Oh…the son of a bitch was studying me earlier. It knew if it could distract me for even a second, it'd get in a blow. And it did. Nothing hard, but, shit, it was being a tricky cockswab. Not that I had a weakness or anything, but damn. Okay, fine, I probably had a weakness and how *dare* that ugly dragon wannabe try to exploit it.

I rushed forward and sliced two of its front legs in half. The air painted silver, I ducked and jabbed the arm blade upward. The creature screamed. I backed off, assessing the situation before going in for the kill. The blood burned away from the visor enough to show…

"What the actual shit?"

Once again, I lost the spiderdragon. The floor, too slathered with blood, I couldn't even follow a trail. Damn it, Clusterfuk. You let it get—GAH.

There I went thinking in the third person again.

I need a vacation.

Preferably not Australia, but probably Australia. I kinda missed those cunts. Even Paul, the bloodiest cunt of'em all.

So, again, I searched the stupid core room for the spiderasshole.

Didn't take me long the second time around.

I found it slipping and sliding in blood, trying to get up. With the severed legs, it was having a hell of a time too. I grinned, walked around to where its head whipped back and forth. When it saw me, it squeaked. Like a mouse. So weird.

"Hey, bruh." I hunkered down in front of it while it scrambled helplessly in all the blood. Finally, it plopped down, splashing me. I sighed. "You know how much dry cleaning a suit like this cost? More than your life, mister." I tapped its smoldering muzzle. It grunted, though I could tell in its hazy eyes it was done. It had no more fight left.

I stared at the monster for some time. Not sure why, just did. During that short time, I watched its red eyes fade to pink. A gurgle bubbled in its throat. The smoke swirling out its nostrils dissipated. And, for just a moment, I saw something in those pink eyes. Like it desperately wanted to tell me something but couldn't. Its maw opened, snapped shut. A low rumble came from deeper in its body.

Slowly, its head lowered into the blood. A long breath jetted from both nostrils. Then its eyes closed, and it breathed no more.

I stood, gave the creature a light nudge with the tip of my boot. Nothing. It was dead.

What was it trying to tell me, anyway? It appeared to be something very important the way it struggled.

Such was my life.

Right when I thought I was about to learn something cool…boom…nothing. Meh. Whatever.

I walked away from the final dead spiderdragon and stopped at the core. According to Asshole Jeff, there was a crystal that powered the core. But, to my knowledge, cores were self-sustaining once activated. So, what the hell was the crystal, or element, for? What purpose did it…

Finally, it sunk in.

It turned cores into rifts, or portals. It allowed creatures from other dimensions into ours. What the actual fuck did Jeff want to do with it? I mean, that scared me a little. Not really. But, it did make me think that Jeff had more at stake than just bringing a few survivors home or exterminating alien bugs on a popular station in the Hob Galaxy.

Yup. He was totally the cliché villain. He wanted the crystal for power or profit and was willing to send a team (thankfully, I went instead, because, damn). Only problem…where the shit was the crystal?

"You need help?" Seri called from the high landing.

"No," I shouted. "Aren't you supposed to be finding a way off the station, or something?"

I made my way around the massive core, searching for signs of a power source and coming up empty. Where the shit would some weird power crystal be hidden, anyway? Felt like maybe Jeff was messing with me until I spotted a flickering blue light just above the core. Just a glimpse, but there. I stepped back, commanding my visor to zoom in.

"I thought you might need some help," Seri said, suddenly behind me.

"Jesus fuck *knuckles*," I said, spinning around. "Why do you keep doing that shit?"

She frowned. "Doing what?"

I waved a dismissive hand. "Never mind. I need you to reboot the systems and get your asses to the pods. Set course for…um…" Took me a second or two to think of a slightly less hostile planet within pod distance. Those little balls of sweet lovin' only had enough sub-nuclear power to reach about six light years away before system failures. Trust me, I about kicked the bucket a few times by miscalculating distances. Finally, a planet besides the one I offered before came to me. The other one was too close. Jeff would have people there.

"Galut," I finished.

Her frown deepened. "Why not the one you told us before?"

"Because, my employer will be there and you'll all fuckin' die, okay? Trust me on this."

Seri's face drooped a bit. "Isn't Galut a scum planet?"

"Listen here, my lil' discrimination princess, beggars can't be choosers right now."

Her shoulders slumped. Defeated. "Fine. I think I can figure out how to reboot it."

"Good deals. You do that. I…have something I need to find."

She cocked an eyebrow. "Like what?"

I pointed at the flickering blue light above the core. Barely visible unless one really stopped and looked. "Like that. My employer wants the crystal."

Seri fell silent for a bit before she said, "You know that's illegal, right?"

"Yeah, well, no one said I was a legal exterminator. Get to work, hun. Once you're all out, I'll pull the plug."

"I should arrest you."

I laughed. "Okay. I mean, you can try. Might not end well, though."

"I—"

"I'm trying to save you people," I said. "Why can't you get that through your thick skulls? I'm not a hero, but not a monster either. Get shit going and get out of here as quickly as possible."

She opened her mouth, I wasn't sure what for and I held up a hand.

"Nope. Be gone, foul one!"

"But—"

"No."

"I just—"

"Piss off."

Seri appeared undecided. Like, either shoot me with her laser pistol or do what needed to be done. Totally conflicted for a few seconds. Finally, though, she nodded and hurried away toward the command center.

Meanwhile, I glared at the tiny blue flicker above the core, hating life.

God, I could go for a super burrito supreme doused in cheese sauce right then.

I blinked. Shook my head.

Focus, jacknuts.

I didn't have enough power to antigravity to the thing. And, as far as I could tell, the arcs over the core didn't appear thick enough to climb. Lovely. So, what the hell was I supposed to do?

I mean, there was a way to charge the suit, but it would take forever without an Elite powering dock. Like days. There had to be a way up to the blue flickering thing. I mean, *someone* put it there, right? It didn't just float like a fairy and…

"I'm an idiot."

My gaze happened on a small bucket lift not far from the core. I ran to the lift, climbed into the bucket, and took a second or two to figure out the controls. Simple enough. At least I didn't have to move the damn thing outside of the bucket. It was all right there.

I pressed the green start button. It whirred to life under me. The bucket vibrated a moment before falling still.

"Easy, fella," I said, and maneuvered the lift as close to the core as I could.

The core itself was probably about eighty yards in diameter, a stormy ball of energy. Getting too close could be bad. Melt through the suit and roast me like a Thanksgiving turkey bad. Slow and tasty.

Wait…

I shook my head and focused on controlling the lift. I rose higher and higher. The flickering became slow, glowing pulses. The crystal itself wasn't something I expected either. I imagined something long and slender with a broad tip and—wait. No. Not that. Pervs. C'mon. I meant like the cliché kind of crystal. Ya know? Like…gah, never mind. It wasn't like the stereotypical crystal, okay? Shut up.

The crystal was a cluster.

Yeah, that's right, bitches. A total CLUSTER. *Wink-wink.*

Anyway, shards poked out of a blue base. At least twenty. All pointy and long. They—

Goddamn it. How the shit was I supposed to make it all sound *not* sexual? Guess it was my cross to bear. Or something.

Once the height was right, I reached out for the crystal, stopping myself at the last second. It hovered about fifty feet above the core. What held it in the air like that? What—

The red squiggles directly below me parted. What the shit? A low thrum vibrated through the suit. If the lift shook, I didn't notice. The yellowish-orange core split open and what crawled out of it was beyond anything I could comprehend at first.

Not a spiderdragon, or snakepede. No. What crawled out was something that resembled Bigfoot. Almost primate. Much larger, though. Standing like fifteen feet tall, large. And let's not even think about the six arms and four legs it boasted. Yeah. Let's just kinda bury that fact because, holy shit tits!

It stumbled off the core and collapsed on the floor, massive shoulders heaving with every breath.

I lifted the arm blade, stared at it, and sighed.

Shutting down the core was imperative to stop the influx of interdimensional creatures. At the same time, I needed to take care of the six-armed Bigfoot thing before Seri rebooted the station so the survivors could get out. Once I knew all the pods were deployed, I planned on rigging the station to blow and use my pod to escape, if possible.

Easier said than done, though.

I wasn't a hero, but letting people die on the Uris Station was just evil.

They deserved a fighting chance.

"How's it going, Seri?" I shouted.

She popped out of the command center. With her angle, she couldn't see the abomination that crawled out of the core, or rift. Whatever.

"It's rebooting. Just a few minutes. I think."

"Lovely," I said and returned my attention to the six-armed Bigfoot, which staggered to its feet. It glanced around, utterly confused. To her, I said, "Stay in the command center. Get it all worked out. Don't check on me, just go and get the others in pods and get the fuck off this heap of scrap metal."

She didn't say anything for a long time.

"You understand?" I asked.

"Y-Yes. Sorry. What about you?"

I loved the thought but didn't let her know it. Not how I worked. Regardless how I felt, I wasn't a goddamn hero. I was far from moral or honorable. I shouldn't even exist, if one were to think about it.

What if I really died the night the snakepede broke into our home and I've just been stuck in some weird Purgatory?

"I'll be fine, sweet cheeks. Promise. Now, go."

When she finally stopped responding, I lowered the bucket and jumped out. The Bigfoot creature, back facing me like a wall of black fur, rose to its full height. And, holy King Kong, the bastard was huge. Okay, not quite King Kong big, but close enough. The fucker was big, okay? I didn't have any shield. Kind of intimidating.

What? Oh, I see. Y'all thought since I was Clink Clusterfuk: Badass of the Cosmos I would just go at that big, hairy bastard like a drunk prom date. Eh, or something like that. Okay, not like that. Sickos. Drag your minds out of the gutter for a second, huh? I mean, what would you do if a forty-foot Bigfoot with six arms towered over you?

Run and hide?

Yup.

#metoo.

A brief squeal echoed throughout the core room. All the lights flickered on. The core gave off a loud hum. The vibration alone forced me to stumble away. Even in the Elite suit. All the normal motor functions were fully operational, including the stabilizers. Regardless, I stumbled. So did the Bigfoot-like monster.

It actually dropped to its knees for a moment while Uris Station came back to life.

I hurried away from it, creating some distance to work with, and shouted, "Hey! You six-armed freak!"

It spun facing me, massive shoulders rising and falling with every breath. Did I mention Bigfoot, or apish? Heh. Yeah, no. Seeing its face for the first time tossed all that shit out the window. There wasn't anything at all resembling Bigfoot, or even an ape. Its face boasted a long, black, serrated beak. Its green eyes narrowed on me. The rest of the face was something out of a Lovecraft story. Total madness. Absolute chaos. Small, orange tentacles wriggled from the creature's cheeks. Ashen horns, at least six, spotted its forehead.

The rest of the beast was all Bigfoot-like. Broad, no doubt heavily muscled under all that heavy fur. Instead of mere hands, though, I spared a glance at the large claws. Long, pointy nails the color of rust sprouted from the fingertips. Claws that could rip me apart in no time. Even in the Elite suit. Claws sharp enough and strong enough to lay waste to the entire, vast, station in a matter of a couple hours.

Yeah. I had a feeling the bastard was fuckin' fast too. Not sure why. I leaned on the hunch. Something I leaned on a lot over the years. Never failed me, either.

Its green eyes narrowed to slits, long beak parting wide in a thunderous roar I felt through the suit. It even made me stagger back a few steps. More ashen spikes rose out of the creature's fur on it shoulders and split the skin of its knuckles. It lumbered toward me. All four legs moved with uncanny grace. So much so, I wasn't sure if I could outmaneuver the thing.

Without a gun, I felt utterly worthless. Stupid arm blade and its stupid non-shooting abilities. I was basically nothing right then.

I'd been mostly unarmed dozens of times and didn't die. Though, I never encountered giant monsters during those times either. The aliens or bugs were relatively small so I could rip and slice my way through.

The Bigfoot shifted and I darted to the left. It didn't attack, however. Just watched me move, green eyes still narrowed. Its beak clacked shut, head titled to the side as though trying to figure out what the hell I was up to.

I paused, frowned.

Why wasn't it coming after me?

I swallowed down a lump and tentatively moved closer to it. Not too close, though. "Uh…so, how's it hangin'?"

Its eyes relaxed a bit. The squinty glare dissolved. A soft chirp emerged from its beak. All the tension appeared to melt away from the monster. Its shoulders slumped some.

"So, um, do you talk or…?"

Its head titled to the other side. And, Christ tossin' thumbtacks at a gargoyle, was it purring? It didn't say anything, though. Not that I really expected it to. The big guys, in most species anyway, rarely talked. All I ever got were grunts and slobber. So, I didn't—

"Yes."

I blinked, glanced around. My gaze found the creature again. "Was that you?"

It nodded. "Yes." It was more like a hiss than speech and not verbal speech.

"Oh, lovely. You're a telepath."

It nodded again. "Yes."

"Is that all you know how to say, or…?"

"No."

I sighed and pointed at the Ethinian crystal. "Okay, well, I need to get that crystal and be on my way."

It spared a glance, looked at me, shook its head. "No."

"The shit you mean, 'no'? It's not up for debate Big Ugly."

"I do not like your tone," the monster spoke in my mind.

"Yeah, well, maybe you shouldn't have come here, right? I mean, rifts are big no-nos. You don't just go checkin'em out. Unless you're stupid."

Those green eyes narrowed again. "You call me stupid?"

I nearly spit with my snort. "With an answer like that, uh…yes. Yes, you're an idiot."

Tension rippled through the beast. All six claws splayed at the thing's sides, fingers waggling. A growl rumbled in its thick throat.

Ah, there it was. Every species had its tipping point.

"Look at me. I'm a big, dumb, hur-hur," I said, mentally face-palming. And yet, "I went through a rift because I'm a durbadur and can't think. I'm just a—"

Its beak shot open, expelling a loud roar.

"Oops," I said. "Here we go." I hurried away from it, arm blade ready.

"I wanted peace," the monster shouted in my mind. "I wanted to learn from you. But you are not worthy!"

Still backing away, I laughed. "Okay, Medieval infomercial."

Fuck it.

The monster roared and lunged for me. I jumped away, lashing out with the arm blade and missing. It slunk away, though all six arms were spread wide, claws ready to shred. Its beak snapped at me.

Yeah, I needed to be careful now. That thing could literally break me open and slurp my intestines up like spaghetti. I didn't doubt its strength, nor its speed. Never underestimate an enemy, in other words.

It came at me again with all three right arms, which I dodged easily until the left arms swept into action. Wasn't expecting that shit. They caught me hard, sending me pinwheeling through the air until I struck a small shed-like building.

Okay, that sucked fuzzy donkey balls. The suit might have taken minimal damage, but inside…ouch. Might as well have been punched in the stomach, chest and back by a professional boxer. My entire body hurt. I staggered away from the metal shed-thing and shook my head.

"Okay," I said. "Now you've gone and done it. You fucked with the wrong—*eeeee!*"

It came out of nowhere and smacked me a second time. Once more, I cartwheeled through the air and crashed into some small building or another. Once more, my body became a pillar of pain.

MINIMAL DAMAGE, the visor read.

Well, that was just fantastic, wasn't it? Ugh. Agony hissed out of my mouth when I stood. Christ, I felt like an old dude suffering arthritis, or something. I lifted my head just in time to receive yet another blow from the jacked up Bigfoot creature.

And, there I went, tumbling through the air with the greatest of ease.

Crash.

MINIMAL DAMAGE.

That last one really banged me up. I was gonna be one giant bruise if I made it out of the situation alive. A notion I gradually began to accept. It was too strong. Too fast.

Throbbing in agony, I stood, swayed and blinked at the monster storming toward me. A mountain of black fur, claws and snapping beak. If it kept smacking me around like that, I wouldn't make it. Sooner or later I'd get a head injury. Then it'd be game over, motherfuckers.

Teeth gritted in pain, I lifted the arm blade. "Okay, you ugly cunt. Let's dance."

Its beak opened, expelling a massive roar I felt even through the suit. There was no time to think. No time to plan. It loomed over me like an ominous thunderhead. It didn't strike right away, but I was done taking chances. Should've killed the bastard from the get-go.

Despite the pain, I sprinted to the right, narrowly avoiding another swipe of three claws. Gods, the power in those hits were jarring. If I had a gun, it'd be a mound of twitching blood and fur, but…

It swung at me again. I rolled away, barely avoiding the blow. I popped up, jumped over one of the large arms, and spotted my opening. I lunged but the bastard moved before the arm blade could plunge into its broad chest.

"Damn it," I said and readjusted my position several feet away from the beast.

I shouldn't let it regain composure. Indeed, I should've used an arm and jumped. I should've slashed its throat open. It wasn't fear that stilled me, however, but a need to know my enemy. Too late to try and talk to it now. That time had passed. But I needed to know its motives.

I didn't buy that it accidently stumbled through a rift. It was too damn intelligent for that.

An idea occurred to me.

"You're their boss, aren't you." Not a question.

It stopped, claws inches from me. I stepped aside.

"Yeah, I thought so. It wasn't an accident you came through the rift. You're their goddamn leader."

The monster attacked, full force. I darted right, missing a claw or two. It swung around with a wall of claws. Literally all three left arms blocked my view of everything else.

"Okay, motherfucker," I said and swept the arm blade. Blood the color of cheap red wine sprayed as the blade sunk deep into one of the wrists.

It wailed and smacked me away like an annoying fly. I tumbled away, sprang to my feet. The creature held its spurting wrist. Thick grunts spewed from its throat and out its beak. A beak that opened and closed, opened and closed. Already, its blood mixed with the rest. Silver and red, now scarlet.

I sprinted at the big bastard, ready to give the killing blow.

The beast snapped a glare at me. A roar blasted out that ridiculous beak. I didn't stop. Shit, I *couldn't* stop. It was do or die now. I roared too, stepped onto a bit of rubble, and leaped into the air like a goddamn Spartan warrior, arm blade cocked back ready to strike. It was moments like that I wished someone would just snap a quick pic, ya know? I mean, c'mon! Look at that badassery right there! It deserved to be immortalized.

That's it. If I ever got out alive, I was gonna hire my own photographer.

Not really.

Okay, really. Probably should've done that years ago. Alas…

The creature didn't have time to bat me away like a mosquito before my blade sank into its shoulder.

Shit, I missed.

I meant to bury the blade into its throat.

I gripped its thick, black fur, yanked the blade free in a spray of blood and crawled onto its shoulder like an angel or devil. It screamed and thrashed. Though it appeared to be in pain because it never reached for me. In fact, it didn't seem to realize I stood on its shoulder. Poor thing, it was in a frenzy of agony.

So, I stroked the fur near its cauliflower ear. I leaned in close. "Shh, darling. We can finally be together now."

Even through the suit, I felt its muscles tense.

"Sorry, cutie. It's not you…it's me." I plunged the arm blade into its throat.

The beast reared, arms flailing. The cry of agony became a muted gurgle. The blade sliced through its throat, emerging just under the bottom jaw in a spatter of blood. Blood which gushed a nanosecond later, then sprayed like a goddamn geyser. I stumbled away from the blast, clutching the fur while the monster went nuts. It tried clapping claws on its throat to stem the bleeding but I'd stick them with my blade every time. It really didn't know who it was fuckin' with. It—

Before my brain caught up to what was happening, I landed flat on my back, most of the wind driven out of me. I laid there, mouth open, trying to inhale and unable to for what felt like decades. Finally, I managed a thin trickle of air. After that, I was breathing okay. Little by little.

The creature sputtered, tried to roar and failed in a gurgling torrent.

I rolled away and stood. Everything hurt. Like, to the point of just giving up ouch. I was one giant fuckin' bruise and, I mean, I had gotten hurt worse, but right then I just—

The monster dropped to its many knees and the floor shook under me. Its hands clasped its throat while blood poured and spurted through its fingers and out its beak. Two quick phist-phist sounds barely drew my attention before I noticed the black, smoldering holes in the monster's forehead.

What the…? I looked up to find Seri on a high landing, steam still curling out of her laser pistol, nodding at me.

The giant monster managed a few thick, bubbly noises, and fell flat on its face. Its beak snapped with the impact.

"Goddamn it," I said, glaring at Seri. "Didn't I tell you to get the fuck outta here?"

She frowned. "I thought you might need some help."

"What the f—when did I ever give you the inkling, I needed help? I told you I got this and to get the hell off the station. Seriously, your listening skills need improvement."

"Fuck you," Seri said. "You wouldn't have made it if I didn't shoot that thing."

"Donkeyshit, lady! I would've—"

Wet squelching sounds drew my attention to the dead creature.

"Would've what?" Seri shouted.

I ignored her, frowning at the corpse. I stepped forward, stopped. Something under the creature's hide moved and bulged. Like billions of boiling maggots. The squelching grew louder. The body itself jerked and appeared to convulse while a large hump formed on its back.

"What. The. Shit?"

I was just beginning to back away when the monster's hide split open, spilling millions of small snake-like creatures out. I mean, it was a fuckin' flood, people. It wasn't until one got close enough that I realized it was snake-like *and* centipede-like.

"Holy shitsuckers," I said. "Snakepedes!"

"What?" Seri's question was so far away.

I really didn't acknowledge except, "Run! Get the fuck outta here!"

Without making sure she left, I ran for the bucket lift and extended it to its full height, which was still a good four feet away from the stupid crystal Jeff wanted.

Fuck it.

I balanced myself on the edge of the bucket and leaned forward. Below, the core roiled and pulsed. If I fell, I'd be less than burnt toast. I'd be incinerated. The baby snakepedes were already crawling into the bucket. Regardless, I needed to get the crystal.

I about fell a couple times because those snaky bastards were creepy as all hell, but with a good stretch, I clutched the flickering blue crystal and slipped back into the bucket. The entire room erupted in alarms telling me I had twenty minutes before total core failure. The bucket took too long so I jumped out and ran for the nearest stairs.

"What'd you do?" Seri asked when I made it to the top catwalk. "We—"

"Get your people. Get to the pods like I told you to do. You have ten minutes. Go!"

She gaped at me.

"Oh, for fuck sake." I turned her to the open doorway behind her and gave her a push. "Go. Your turn to be a hero. Get them off this rusty shit stain."

She glanced over her shoulder, nodded and ran through the doorway.

Great. I hoped she made it to safety. I hoped they all did. And I didn't have time to make sure they did.

My final objective was to get to my pod outside the station, redirect the coordinates to Jeff's station and hope shit worked out. That was all I could do. Hit GO and pucker up to see what happened. There might be a metaphor in there about life, if I was a cynic. Which I wasn't. Yes, I was. Not. Yep. Not. Y—

Oh, for shit sake, my mind was all over the place.

Alarms brayed. At least I had flickering lights to guide me instead of trying to run in the dark. It's the little things, really…

EIGHTEEN

Running through the corridors, not sure where the hell I was on the station, I cradled the cluster crystal like a tight-end twenty yards from the goal line.

I stumbled into a small room. Something thin and pale crouched, facing the far corner. Its bony back expanded with every inhale. A wheezy sigh floated on the air.

"Uh, yeah, no," I said and darted out of the room. Whatever it was, I didn't have time to mess with it, nor did I want to. Fuckin' thing was creepy, yo.

In a narrow hall, I ran as fast as the suit would carry me. If the visor was accurate, I ran about twenty miles per hour. Best I could do with all the twisting and turning and bashing down doors. Not like I had a straight shot to the pod outside.

Also, I hoped the damn thing was still there. And if it was still there, not damaged too much from the bug that tried to bash it to pieces when I first landed, I'd do the Happy Dance before climbing in. Okay, not really. Probably.

The floor quaked under me and the suit compensated for the jostling. How long had I been running? Five minutes? More? Felt like a minute but must be more than that. I didn't know. All I got was ten minutes before the core either blew or imploded.

I bounded up a couple flights of stairs, crashed through closed doors, came across bugs and other creatures pretty much dying from starvation. All of them too weak to do anything other than lift their heads. I ran. The floor shook. The lights burst in sparkling sprays, dousing me in complete black. The suit's lamps flickered on, giving me a fighting chance in the thick stew of darkness.

And let's not forget, I still had no fucking clue where I was. Nothing looked familiar and I wished I would've taken in the scenery better when I entered Uris.

Heh. Entered Uris…

Anyway, yeah, I was pretty much fucked. No way would I find where I needed to go in time. I…

…THIS WAY TO DOCKS.

I paused only a moment at the sign on the wall of the corridor and followed the arrow. Well, shit, paint me a lucky bastard. I wasn't sure where my pod laid, but the docks were a start, right? Sure. Boom, boi!

The docks were made for pods and shuttlecrafts. Nothing huge like the cargo bay would allow. The docks were designed for visitors or potential lifers. Sometimes folks liked living on a station instead of a planet, for some weird-ass reason. They paid for it, of course. Into the millions and more. To say the wealthy chose stations over planets was an understatement.

"You have the crystal?" Jeff spoke into my ear, scaring me.

I jumped. "Don't *do* that shit! Yes, I got your stupid fuckin' crystal."

"Very well. Are you in a pod?"

"Uhh…" I searched the docks for an emergency exit. "Not exactly."

"What do you mean, 'not exactly'?"

"Like I said it, dude. Not exactly. Trying to find a way outside, so can it, eh?"

A pause. Then…

"According to our scans, Uris will explode in three minutes."

"Get bent, Jeff."

"I'm serious, Clusterfuk. You need to—"

"*You* need to shut the hell up, cock stomper, and let me think."

Jeff, thankfully, fell silent.

Soon enough, I found an emergency exit door. I opened it, stepped inside and sealed the door behind me. If Seri and her crew were still aboard, I didn't want to cut their chances shorter than they were already.

Facing the outer door, I drew in a breath, and kicked it open. If not for the suit's clamps, I would've been sucked into space. Hello, Darkness, my old friend and all that silly bullshit.

I ran onto the catwalk and glanced around. To my left, fire billowed out the side of the station.

"Ah, hell," I said and ignored the quaking under my boots as I turned right and followed the catwalk.

The walk dipped, rose, turned and…

"Fuck yeah," I said, spotting my pod.

It rested against a metal I-beam.

There were no sounds in space, but you felt when shit went wrong. I glanced over my shoulder. The station exploded in a massive surge blasting toward me.

I sprinted to the pod, got in, and sat, totally lost. What the shit were the coordinates for Jeff's station? *Fuck.*

Thank all the gods of chunky peanut butter for computer history. I found and redirected the coordinates. The pod quaked. Space didn't allow sound, but the pod did and everything was an explosion.

I slammed a fist on the GO icon. Commanded the suit to open just enough so I held the crystal inside with me and sealed everything up tight.

The pod surged, and—

NINETEEN

"…boarding."

I opened my eyes, squinted through the suit's visor at way too much light, and closed them again.

"The Employer wants him out of the suit and awake before meeting," some dude said.

"Uh-huh," another dude said. "And how do we get the suit off? Elite suits can't be opened from the outside unless cut open."

Right he was. Only way to safely open an Elite suit was for the person inside to command it open. Cutting through it with a torch or saw would probably injure me in some way. I'd heal but, damn it, that shit hurt. I healed, sure, but I still felt pain. I mean, c'mon.

Before they got serious about cutting the suit open, I said, "Open".

Air hissed and the suit parted down the middle like an organic zipper. It split a good three feet apart and stopped. I took my first breath of non-suit air and—

A younger guy stooped over me, recoiled, face wrinkling. "Oof." He waved a hand in front of his face and scrambled away.

"What is it?" Someone I couldn't see asked.

"We might wanna hose him down first."

"What the hell you talking about, Wellis?" An older man loomed over me, craggy face pinched in a frown. "He's just waking u—" His eyes opened wide. His upper lip curled in something like disgust. Finally, he blew out a breath, shook his head. "Get the hose. He pissed himself."

I grinned. Oh, yeah. Right. I peed in the suit. Good times.

Back crackling like fresh cellophane, I stretched and glanced around, finding the two men gaping at me.

"Alright," I said. "Who pissed in the suit while I was sleeping?" I pointed at the younger dude. "It was *you*, wasn't it!"

He blinked, tried to look everywhere but at me. "No. I think you accidently—"

I stood, taking the action slow because the suit took on most of the physical stuff. You got kinda used to it. Then, when there was no suit, you needed to remember how muscles worked. I teetered a bit but didn't topple over like a drunk in the wind. I stretched my back and neck, crackling some more.

"Follow me, Mr. Clusterfuk," the older man said, craggy face disinterested now. "We have a shower, and fresh clothes ready for you."

"Nah," I said. "I'll bring him the crystal like this."

The older man appeared on the verge of a stroke. His right eye twitched.

"Ah, shit," I said. "I just killed ya, didn't I?"

He frowned. "Huh? No. I sincerely request you clean up before your meeting."

"And I sincerely request you eat dildos." I stepped out of the suit, crystal in my hands and walked away.

"Hey—" the younger dude spouted. "You can't do that." A pause. "Can he do that?"

I was a good twenty feet away before the old man replied, "That's Clint Clusterfuk. He can do whatever he wants. C'mon. Let's get the suit cleaned up."

That's fuckin' right, bitches.

I stormed, in all my stinkiness, out of the docking bay and entered the main station. Jeff's station was small, so, I reckoned, I'd eventually find him. Either that or—

"You there," six fully armored guards met me about halfway down the hall. "Where is your…ID… pass…" Whoever spoke (helmets made it difficult to know who the hell was talking half the time) trailed off, apparently recognized me. I spotted him since he was the only one who lowered his weapon. The others remained tensed and ready for action, however.

"Yeah," I said. "You boys should probably point those rifles at each other, or something, and let me through."

"Let's see your ID pass," one of them spouted.

I cocked an eyebrow at no one in particular. "Are you really that stupid? Look, I'm givin' all you wankers five seconds to step aside or you're all dead. Got it?"

Save for one, they all stepped away.

And so, I knew who still insisted on the ID pass. Funny, no one warned the cunt.

I stood a few inches above him. Regardless, anyone in their right mind wouldn't confront a highly trained guard without some form of protection, or gun. I had neither. All I held was the stupid crystal. My reputation and face were enough for most people. But this dude…

"Okay," I said. "I'm gonna give you an extra five seconds to step aside. If you don't, I'll shove that rifle up your ass, kid."

"We have direct orders not to—"

"One."

"Are you crazy? Guys? Why aren't you doing anything?"

"Two."

He nudged the rifle's muzzle at my chest. "Get a pass."

"Three."

He glanced at his fellow guards, who stood, guns lowered, not saying or doing a damn thing. "I'll tell The Employer about you all. He'll—"

"Four."

He stepped back and I stepped forward. "Look, you can't—"

"Five." I snatched the rifle out of his hands, swung low, kicked his feet out from under him, and slammed a boot on to his chest. He gripped my ankle hard enough to hurt. Still, I remained firm. "Well, well, looks like someone really wants a rifle up his ass." I began to turn him over.

He wailed and managed, "No! Ah, God. I'm sorry! Please don't hurt me!"

I favored him with a smirk and tossed the rifle aside. "I'll give you a pass. Just this once. Get outta here."

He scrambled away and I continued toward Jeff's living quarters.

Some guys just needed a little kick in the ass when confronted with an unstoppable force.

Apparently, though, the first team of guards didn't warn the next eight. They all came at me, full force, demanding an ID pass. None of them stepped aside.

"Look," I said. "I'm Clint Clusterfuk. I have the Ethinian crystal. Jeff is all about this crystal too. Like, he probably spanks his monkey dreaming about it. That's how serious this shit is, gentlemen. Now, let me through."

They didn't budge.

"Oh, for fuck sake." I yanked the rifle out of the nearest guard's hands, kicked him away and swung the gun on the other seven.

They all flinched and pointed their guns at me.

I sighed. "Look, I'm tired, horny and desperately in need of a beer. So, like, kindly step outta the fuckin' way, eh."

They didn't move. Didn't speak. All their rifles fixed on me. Well, except for the dude I stole my rifle from. He slunk behind his mates, no doubt pretty damn embarrassed.

I rolled my eyes. "Do I really have to kill all of you?"

Still, they remained steadfast. Such loyal little goons.

I shot three in quick unison. The plasma blasts sheared off most of their heads. Blood splattered and I think one guy screamed. I snorted, kicked the rifle out of another guard's hands and blew a hole in his stomach and—

"Clusterfuk! What the *hell* do you think you are *doing*?"

I turned to the right and found Jeff standing on a flight of narrow stairs. And, oh…he was pissed. His face was a storm about ready to let loose.

I tossed the rifle over my shoulder and extended my arms. "There's Mr. Cutie Britches! Mommy's home!"

The storm that was his face didn't let up. He turned to walk up the stairs. "Follow me."

I spun, flipped the remaining guards off, and hurried to catch up to the big man himself. Which was easier said than done because, hoo-boy, those stairs were steep and all I wanted was a nap and—

Finally, I stumbled through a doorway into a large, dimly lit room.

I stopped, sniffed. "Is that…vanilla incense?"

"Shut up," Jeff said. He stood way too close. Like only three feet away close.

I sidestepped away from him, cocked an eyebrow. "Pretty rude for someone who wants a power crystal held by someone who can kill you whenever he fuckin' feels like it."

The storm on Jeff's face vanished, replaced by complete indifference. "Doubtful, Mr. Clusterfuk. Hand the crystal over." He held out a hand with fingers that were way too long.

"Yeesh, dude. There's surgery for that kind of deformity, ya know? And no. You pay me first."

He chuckled humorlessly, eyes glinting in the soft glow of a nearby lamp. "You are in no position to make demands, Clusterfuk. Hand the crystal over and I will uphold our agreement."

"Ha! I've heard that before. Whaa—whaa. Try again, asshat."

Face still indifferent, Jeff drew a laser pistol and pointed it at me. "I'm not asking. Hand the crystal over or I'll kill you and take it anyway."

A grin spread along my face. "Remember when I called you a cliché villain?"

He frowned. "Yes. Why?"

I swooped in, ripped the pistol from his hand, swung around him and slammed the muzzle against the back of his head. All that, one handed. Good fuckin' gods, I'm good.

"You were doing it again," I said. "The cliché villain thing. Talking too much before actually doing the deed. I mean, c'mon, man."

"If you kill me," Jeff said, "you won't get your money."

I snorted. "You think this is about money? Oh, you adorable piece of shit." I paused long enough for him to begin asking a question and spouted, "Pay me, and you'll have your crystal. I won't even kill you."

He stood there for a long time. Not moving. Not speaking.

Finally, he said, "Fine. The paykey is on my desk." He pointed at an orangewood monstrosity all the way across the room. Because, of course it was all the way across the room.

Gah.

"Well, let's go get that shit, huh?" I nudged the back of his head with the pistol.

Jeff sighed and strode ahead, faster than I anticipated. I jogged a bit to catch up, though never more than five feet away.

We reached the desk and he picked the paykey card up. "This has the exact amount."

"All twenty million?"

"We never agreed on a price. It's ten million."

In order to take the card, I needed to either drop the crystal, or gun. Fuck that noise. Instead, I leaned forward and used my teeth to take the card from Jeff's ugly-ass long fingers.

"Did you just—"

"Yush. Shuh'et." Hard as hell to talk with a card between your teeth. Ya know.

I backed away, pistol still pointed at his head. I hunkered down, placed the crystal on the floor and continued backing away. I took the card out of my mouth and tucked it in a pocket of my piss stained jeans. Ah, Australia. I wore your denim proud.

At the doorway to the stairs, I said, "The crystal is on the floor. Count to ten and it's yours. You turn before ten, I'll kill you. Get it?"

He nodded.

I began counting. "One. Two. Three. Four. Five…"

He didn't move.

I backed down the steps, pistol still aimed at the back of his ugly head. "Six. Seven. Eight…"

Okay, fuck it. I turned and tromped down the steps as fast as I could. When I shot out into the mid-station, a clean-up crew was washing the blood off everything. I snorted. Good times.

I knew what I needed to do. And time wasn't on my side.

I ran like I never ran before until I came to the docking bay where my suit…should've been.

Spinning in a full circle, heart thrumming, I spouted, "The shit? Where'd it go?"

My gaze fixed on a large sanitation chest in a far corner. Yes. Made perfect sense. They would want to clean it and completely revitalize it. Which included charging. Hells yeah!

It took me barely a minute to make it to the long, standing chest when the alarms blared.

"You bastard," I muttered, though knew full well he would double cross me. That was just how those cliché villains worked, ya know?

I opened the chest and was engulfed in steam. Coughing, I backed away and tried to think of a good escape. I didn't know Jeff's station all that well. I was in the back, but not the deployment bay. If there was such a thing. Named differently, probably, but...ya know...

The steam dissipated. I said, "Open". I assumed they changed the voice programing but...

The suit slipped open and gaped like an eager mouth.

"Halt," a voice shouted from behind.

"Fuck off," I said, turned, and backed into the Elite suit. It sealed shut before whoever shouted began shooting.

In the helm, a familiar voice said, "Elite booting systems activated."

Shields were activated once the suit sealed. So, if that fuckwad was still shooting, the shields would be taking care of it.

In a matter of seconds, the visor read: SUIT ACTIVATED. 60% shields. Air quality is stable.

The visor cleared, reveling dozens of guards in front of me.

"Back off," I shouted. They all glanced at each other, so I knew they heard me. Still, none of them moved.

"Fine," I said. "Just remember, I warned ya." They began disbanding, though too late.

I leaped out of the casket and punched out as many as I could before picking up a low grade plasma rifle and blasting a couple of them. They all scattered and I surged forward.

I wasn't done with Jeff yet...

TWENTY

He sat behind his stupid orangewood desk. The crystal rested inches from his long, steepled hands. It pulsed bright blue the closer I came to it.

"What are you doing here?" Jeff asked. "You have been paid."

I barked laughter. Bad guys loved it when I barked laughter (sarcasm). It scared them a little. Once I had him completely unnerved, face slack, eyes wide, I plopped down in the chair across the desk from him. Fully suited, the chair groaned under my weight.

"Pulling the fire alarm doesn't count, Jeffy."

The slackened, wide-eyed expression firmed up into a glower before resting on a humorless grin. If he thought the grin was intimidating, he needed to practice some more in the mirror because…woof.

"Mr. Clusterfuk, you really didn't think I'd let you just stroll out of here after pointing a gun at my head?" He grunted. "Hardly. No. You are done. You are a dishonor to the Military. A dishonor to everything you touch. Even yourself."

I snorted. "Aww, sweetie. How do you know I touch myself?"

His face flashed with anger. There and gone. "I'm doing you a favor, really. Putting an end to your miserable life."

"Miserab—" I leaned forward and pointed a finger at him. "Shut your damn cockhole, motherlicker!"

"Might as well just step outside without the suit. Just give up, Clusterfuk. It's over."

I waved a hand. "Yeah, yeah, Mr. Cliché Villain, whatever. Look, I'm gonna leave now and you're gonna let me leave. If not, everyone in this entire station is gonna die. Got it, Jeffy-Poo?"

He stood, trying to appear all menacing and scary. Jaw clenched. Eyes all squinty. Heh. FAIL. I stood too, and in the suit I towered over him. I triggered the arm blade and brandished it at him.

"Okay," I said. "You want this shit to come out bloody? Because this is how you shit blood, pal."

For the first time, true fear trickled across his face. I smiled and stepped closer. My legs bumped his desk. The crystal toppled over with a clunk.

Jeff backed away, held up his laser pistol. "My High Guards are coming. They will kill you, even in that suit."

"High, eh? And why aren't they fuckin' sharin'?" I reached across the desk, grabbed Jeff by the throat, and lifted him into the air. He gagged, mouth open, tongue wagging. His eyes bulged from their sockets.

I pulled him in close. "I'll let you in on a little secret, homeslice." I paused, because effect was everything. "I wasn't planning on letting you live anyway."

He gagged, blinking.

I snatched up the crystal with my free hand and slammed the sharp ends into Jeff's head. He convulsed; blood trickled from his nose. His eyes rolled up to reveal only the whites. I dropped the evil bastard onto his desk and exited the room. Some men, alien or not, just deserved to die.

The crystal didn't matter to me either. I could probably pawn it off somewhere for a nice price, but, honestly, I was over it. Time to move on to bigger and better things, for shit sake. I tromped down the narrow stairway and emerged to the main station. There were no guards. Nothing. Everyone was either too afraid, or ill equipped.

So, I strolled through the station without any confrontation. Until I found the small deployment bay, anyway. There, I was met with some bullshit. Because, there were always rando assholes ready to throw down for no reason.

"The fuck ya doin'?" a big, dark haired dude spouted once I entered the bay.

He wore greasy, blue denim overalls and a sloped brow. I imagined Neanderthal in overalls and laughed. I mean, c'mon. One couldn't make that shit up sometimes. I continued toward him and the four goobers behind him sporting similar overalls and big wrenches in their hands.

I didn't want to kill them. Give me that much credit, at least. But when they all battered me with those wrenches, spouting racial slurs…enough was enough. In a single, swift sweep of the arm blade, I severed all five heads. Blood splattered my visor though quickly burned off. Damn, they really knew how to charge an Elite suit. At only sixty percent, it was fuckin' perfect.

I found a sturdy pod, climbed in and sealed it. I was about to set the coordinates and stopped.

An idea floated to the surface of my mind. I exited the pod and rushed to the station's core, which wasn't very far from the bay, to my surprise.

The orange core pulsed sporadically with certain energy demands.

No crystal above that one. Not that it mattered.

I found the command center, knocked the guy out manning shit, and set all the gauges to high. There was probably a failsafe, but…it was worth a try.

Back at the pod, I sealed in and tapped in my desired coordinates.

Would Jeff's station blow up? Shit, I didn't know.

Would it create an utter Clusterfukery?

Fuck yeah.

I wasn't even sure if the coordinates were correct. If not…I'd be hurtled into the sun. Sometimes we just needed to take risks.

Even through the intakes, I took in the pod's air. Filtered or not, I…

TWENTY-ONE

I dreamed about Seri from the Uris Station. I wondered about her crew. Did they make it? Gods of wrinkly nuts, I hoped so. I…

"Fuckin' hell," A familiar voice boomed through my dreams. "Not this cunt again."

My eyelids fluttered, though were too heavy to open fully.

"Maybe we're all he's got," another, though soothing voice said.

"Who opened the suit?" Yet another familiar voice spouted. This one sounding much older.

Was my suit open? I didn't know. Nor did I give a shit. My eyelids drooped in weariness. I just didn't care about anything. Sleep. Sleep was what mattered.

Faint, but there, someone said, "Welcome back, Clusterfuk, ya ugly cunt."

I smiled, vison clearing.

Paul shook his head and said…

"Get up, ya fuckin' wanker. We got roos to kill."

Finally, I was home.

THE END

SEVERED**PRESS**

facebook.com/severedpress
twitter.com/severedpress

CHECK OUT OTHER GREAT SCIENCE FICTION BOOKS

LOST EMPIRE
by Edward P. Cardillo

Building on their victory in the last Intergalactic War, the imperialist United Intergalactic Coalition seeks to expand their influence over the valuable Kronite mines of Golgath. Reeling from their defeat, the warrior Feng are down but not out. The overextended UIC and the vengeful Feng deploy battle groups and scramble fighters as they battle for position in the universe, spinning optics and building coalitions. Captain Reinhardt of the Resilience and the elite Razor's Edge squadron uncover the Feng Emperor Hiron's last ditch attempt to turn the tables with a new and dangerous technology. With resources spread thin, the UIC seeks to exploit Feng's weakened position through a very conditional peace accord. Unwilling to submit, Emperor Hiron must hold them off and quell the growing civil unrest of his starving, warrior people just long enough to execute the mysterious Operation: Catalyst. Commander Massa and his Razor's Edge squadron race against time to stop Hiron's plan, and a new race awakens, led by a powerful prophet set on toppling the established galactic order through violent acts of terrorism.

ABSOLUTE ZERO
by Phillip Tomasso

When a recon becomes a rescue . . . nothing is absolute!

Earth, a desolate wasteland is now run by the Corporations from space stations off planet . . . A colony of thirty-three people are part of a compound set up on Neptune. Their objective is mining the planet surface for natural resources. When a distress signal reaches Euphoric Enterprises on the Nebula Way Station, the Eclipse is immediately dispatched to investigate.

The crew of the Eclipse had no idea what they were getting themselves into. When they reach Neptune, and send out a shuttle party, they hope they can find the root cause behind the alarm. Nothing is ever simple. Something sinister lies in wait for them on Neptune. The mission quickly goes from an investigation into a rescue operation.

The young crew from the Eclipse now finds themselves in the fight of their lives!